The Light
By Travis Griffith

For the Universe
Thank you for being my light

I'll always love you... to the moon and back

Chapter 1
The End
Monday, February 13, 2006

His mother used to say that light always follows the dark.

"Look for the sunrise, Honey," she'd say in an attempt to comfort young Calvin Janek as he trembled under the sheets from his fear of the dark, "And remember that the darkness is only temporary."

Calvin took solace in his mother's words and closed his tired eyes each night, anxious for the dark to pass and excited to welcome the glow of another morning. He tried his hardest to keep his eyes closed until he sensed the first rays of sunlight silently bursting through the uncovered window.

Calvin remembered his mother's words as an adult, but they seemed ever more distant and had lost the magic of childhood innocence.

The dark of those long ago nights now matched the darkness that had engulfed 28-year-old Calvin's soul and reduced his once-vibrant light to a mere shimmer; a flicker from a dying candle inside an otherwise lightless room.

Anger replaced hope. Fear replaced love. Arrogance replaced faith. Where laughter once reigned, pessimism now thrived.

Calvin desperately wanted out of his darkness before the inevitable death of that last shimmer of light.

His mother's words echoed through his consciousness and he knew he had to stand alone in his dark, at least for a while, if the light of a new dawn were to ever rediscover him.

That's why, on this night, Calvin needed his wife to understand why, after nearly seven years of marriage and two children, he had to leave her.

He just couldn't say the words to her face.

If he tried to explain in person, he'd only stutter through his words and trip over his explanations, making things worse instead of better.

Going back to his comfortable office, where he worked as a creative director at an ad agency, seemed like a safer and more efficient idea. While there he could carefully orchestrate his words into an eloquent and rationally written explanation of why he had the overwhelming desire to leave everything he'd always known.

At 10 p.m., after wrapping production on a video shoot, he retreated to the quiet solitude of his office. That's where much of the previous three months of magic had unfolded. It's in his private 150 square-foot office where he learned so many of the life lessons that brought him to this point. It's there where he battled his demons, both figuratively and literally, and kept his flicker of light alive.

By 2 a.m., after reflecting on those magnificent events that changed his outlook on life forever, he completed the letter.

Before heading home to what he hoped was a sleeping household, he printed the letter and read it one more time while remembering the night that started it all.

The night he met Elizabeth.

Chapter 2
The Beacon Awakens
Wednesday, November 23, 2005

Calvin's evening had gotten off to a strange start. The TV commercial his ad agency was commissioned to shoot was a week past deadline. Being Thanksgiving weekend, Calvin didn't want to be on set any more than the cameraman, producers, actors, and extras did.

But the work had to get done or nobody got paid. The one positive to this shoot, in Calvin's eyes at least, was the attractive blonde who showed up as an extra. Calvin was pretty sure he'd seen her before but couldn't make a connection as to when. She had shoulder-length golden hair, a bubbly personality, a radiant smile, and magnetic eyes. She interacted with almost everyone in the room that night, but didn't seem to give a second glance to Calvin.

As happy and radiant as the woman seemed, Calvin felt a certain pang of sadness, even pity, the more he looked at her; feelings that tugged against the waves of attraction she naturally demanded. He tried to focus his attention elsewhere while fighting a growing temptation to speak with her.

"Cut!" Calvin yelled after wrapping the first scene of the night. He directed his crew to set lighting for the next scene, and used the downtime to follow his compulsion. Against his better judgment, Calvin approached the woman who silently required his attention.

Calvin's rational mind hoped his intent on approaching this woman was simple flirtation but the imagery in his head warned of something deeper.

This type of thing was way out of character for Calvin. Not shy by any means, he wasn't one to strike up a conversation like the one he was about to have with people he didn't know.

He approached as she flashed an already familiar smile and he casually introduced himself.

"Hi, I'm Calvin Janek, the agency's creative director. Thanks for coming tonight."

"Hi Calvin, I'm Elizabeth," she said, shaking his hand. "Nice meeting you!"

There was neither immediate electric shock nor sudden vision, but Calvin knew his purpose in speaking with her. He chose not to broach the subject yet.

"So, are you just looking to meet some new friends tonight?" she asked sarcastically.

He laughed.

"Yeah, I heard that if you're looking for friends, you just assemble a group of people under the guise of a TV shoot on the night before a holiday weekend. Seems as good of a place as any, right?"

"Oh, so you're a sarcastic sassy pants, huh? I like that," she said with a wink and a sly smile.

With the ice broken, they talked during breaks, even flirted with their eyes as the cameras rolled. Feeling more comfortable with her, he worked up the nerve to ask her the question that had burned since shaking her hand.

"Elizabeth, so...um... Okay, I've never done anything like this before... so this might, well... this WILL sound really weird so I am going to just throw it out there."

"Okay..." Elizabeth replied, intrigued.

"Have you recently lost someone; someone who was close to you?"

Elizabeth didn't react the way Calvin thought most people probably would have. Instead, she just looked at him in a most unusual way, not unlike a wide-eyed child marveling at a full moon.

Then she replied simply and matter-of-factly, "Yes, I have."

Maybe it wasn't strange for him to ask her that question at all, but more of a curiosity.

Her answer broke the dam and he couldn't hold anything else back.

"Um, okay. A girl? Tall ...dark hair?"

He didn't know how he knew that, but he could see her in his mind's eye; a transparent, floating image of the young woman. The girl in his vision glanced at him, smiled, took off running, and vanished.

He added, "Was she a runner?"

Elizabeth's expression changed from that of mild curiosity, to one of shock. She walked to the staging area to grab her purse. Calvin refrained from following.

Walking back toward him, she said, "I have a picture of her."

Opening her wallet, she took out what appeared to be a picture of a college sorority. At least 20 young women were in the photograph, but to Calvin, it might as well have been a portrait of one. She stood out immediately and obviously. He pointed directly to the dark-haired, slender woman in the second row, just to the right of center.

He didn't need a verbal confirmation to know that he was right. The look on Elizabeth's face answered for her.

"Yes," she said, nodding and wiping away a tear as it rolled down her cheek, "Her name is Ellis."

"Was... Ellis."

Elizabeth paused for a few seconds before composing herself, then giggled.

"Calvin, you and I just might be long-lost evil twins!"

The way she digitally flipped back to her funny, flirty self slightly disturbed him but also put him at ease. Plus, the thought of having some kind of connection to this girl thrilled him.

"Long lost evil twins, huh? Well, you never know!"

"Okay Calvin! We're ready," the cameraman's voice snapped them both back to the task at hand.

He handed her a business card, then turned his attention back toward the group to address them all, "We're ready to get going again everyone. Let's get this shoot done!"

Chapter 3
The Letter
Tuesday, February 14, 2006

The memory of meeting Elizabeth, and the spiritual events that transpired in the months since, convinced Calvin that his letter had been written with pure intent and conveyed his deepest truth. He hoped reading it would ease Lisa's mind and help her understand his decision.

"I love you Lisa. I loved our happy times, I love seeing you interact with our kids. Yet I have issues right now.

At my core, I can't settle and be complacent. Why? Because that's easy.

Yes, I can handle any pain and deal with the void of staying complacent. It's so much harder to be true to myself and consider leaving, because it hurts so many others.

I've always been about keeping people happy, without regards to my own happiness. That can't go on forever. Not if WE both are to continue growing as people.

I've been submerging myself into the distractions of work, and I think that's also caused me to neglect being the father I should have been all this time.

For a long time I have felt a sucking void deep in me. It has caused me to search far and wide for the ifs, for the might-be's, for the maybes.

I've discovered over the last few months that what I've been missing is growth, and knowing the true concept of love and light. I've missed knowing the act of living and experience. I've missed opportunities of actually LIVING a life, not just walking blindly, consuming food and air to make it to the next day.

By living the life I have been for the past few years, the void has grown daily.

And please understand that when I speak of the true concept of love and light, I do not mean me loving another person. That is not what I am looking for.

I mean loving myself, finding the strength, light, and compassion that I know is in me.

Once that happens, I know I'll find my true love and finally emerge into a new world of light.

Many, if not all, of the answers to life's questions will end in either love or fear. For the last few years my decision to not tell you that I'm unhappy was a result of fear. Fear of life without you, fear of hurting you, fear of you hating me and never wanting to see me again.

But when you remove fear and remove restriction, you find liberating truth and love.

The key is ME being truly happy in order to help my children reach a life of being truly happy as well.

A life without the void. That's what I strive for.

This is what I want to do in my life...spread the knowledge and example of true love and existence. To show the world what it means to experience, to love, to truly LIVE.

If I touch even one life I have done my job in existing.

And just think, there are two lives that came from you and me that we will touch day in and day out for the rest of our lives.

To make a machine work properly when it is broken, you must strip it down component by component until you find the gear that isn't going into place.

We examine and we try and we test until we find the faulty piece.

We either fix it by replacing it, mending it, or in some cases we decide it's not fixable at all. In the same manner I need to find the components, in me and in us, that aren't working and examine them.

It all comes back to my question to myself: Is a life that's comfortable worth sticking with if it leaves me with a void of growth, of pure love... of true happiness?
If I do leave, am I guaranteed to find those things?
No.
Maybe the void is just knowing I've settled with my life.
Maybe void isn't even the right word.
So then the question would be rephrased, "Am I content with settling with my life?"
And regardless of my answer to that, are YOU satisfied knowing I settled?
You are a good person, and have done nothing wrong.
So let me lay this out before you:
I am not being fair to:
You
or my children
Or myself.
Not being fair to the children: mild because they will always love me and I them.
Not being fair to you: huge because it's been so many years of settling for what's comfortable.
Not being fair to me: Profound.
No way around it, if we separate, there will be hurt now, a year from now, 10 years from now.
I need to take care of my situation or it will affect my career.
It will affect my being, my attitude, my heart.
If we do nothing, the situation will be the same now as in ten years, if not worse. I mean, compare my feelings of doubt at 20 to my feelings now. They've amplified.
But if these are aspects I am willing and comfortable to deal with then by all means, I should do it and stay comfortable.

I am torn, confused, scared, and terrified of losing you while at the same time scared of a new life alone.

I still question every once in a while if this can all be true, the happenings of the last three months.

Though I know too many things have happened to be coincidence. I've always been a skeptic, though this time, I believe everything.

I just want to live a life I am at peace with. So many people will say 'Calvin, what the hell are you thinking? You're giving up a wife, everyday life with your amazing children, and for what? Because you aren't completely happy ALL the time? Well no one is! That's life! And you've got it good.'

I can hear it now. People will say that to me, but they don't understand. And I don't think I can make them understand. But as long as I speak the truth always, how can I falter?

I am taking myself down to truth, and struggling to open my eyes and see, as all humans do.

What I do with that truth is free will at its best.

Chapter 4
The Fax
Monday, November 28, 2005

Calvin wished getting out of bed was as easy as falling into it. The night had been fitful and sleepless, which he partially attributed to the strange smear of blue light he saw at about 2 a.m.

It hung slightly to the left of the television, which sat across from the foot of the bed. It lasted only a few seconds and reminded him of a reflection of water, but about as tall as an adult human.

A surge of adrenaline had coursed through his body when he saw it, not able to tell if it was a reflection from the TV, some sort of light coming in from the windows, or something different entirely.

He closed his eyes tightly and willed himself, unsuccessfully, to fall back asleep.

Morning came with a feeling of extreme sluggishness. Even a hot shower did little to lift his mind from the foggy submerged land of disjointed visions and dreams.

Coffee, even in the form of a triple mocha, barely lifted his head to the surface.

Work had been such a pain lately that he blamed part of his energy drain on the fact that he no longer cared about the success of his clients. They had become high maintenance and unusually demanding. He wondered why they wouldn't just let him do what they hired him to do, without complaint.

Calvin had a knack for writing effective TV commercials, and could get a concept into production in a timely manner. When he cared enough about his work, there was no one better. However, it seemed lately most clients wanted to not only tell him what to write, but pick the talent and produce the spots too. When the commercials didn't generate results, clients were quick to unload all responsibility onto him. Most days, it led to spending hours persuading his clients that his style would be far more effective for their marketing campaign. It didn't take him long to realize that people think they're experts in advertising just because they watch TV.

The desk phone rang and Calvin swore before answering it, sure it was another client ready to make unreasonable demands. He answered anyway.

"Hi Kate," he said to the receptionist.

"Yeah Calvin, you have a call from a woman named Elizabeth. She says that she met you last week at a commercial shoot, that she was an extra. Are you available to take the call?"

Just her name had a bigger effect on his heart and mind than the hot shower and three shots of espresso.

"Sure go ahead and transfer her."

It wasn't unusual to receive calls from people who had been extras in commercials. Usually they called to express thanks and convey their hope to land a bigger part. He halfway wondered if that's why Elizabeth had called.

"Hi Elizabeth, Calvin here. How are you?"

"Hi. So sorry to bother you at work, but I really needed to talk to you. Do you have a couple of minutes?"

In truth, he didn't, but a break from clients sounded pretty good and her urgency demanded his attention.

"Sure, what's up?"

"You got a fax this morning," she said, skipping the small talk and getting right to her point.

He thought there obviously must be a mistake, and said, "A fax? What are you talking about? Do people even still send faxes?"

"Calvin, listen to me. It's....it's from Ellis," said Elizabeth hesitantly.

He sat silent for what felt like a minute.

"Ummm... okay..." he said in disbelief, "Just... hang on for a minute.... What?"

He paused again, trying to figure out how to handle this and get more information out of her. His first thoughts were that she was pulling a fast one on him. He briefly considered hanging up the phone.

"You mean Ellis, your friend who died? What are you talking about? That doesn't make any sense."

"Calvin, please, this is so bizarre to me too and I'm trying not to bawl or freak out. You got a fax. Or rather WE got a fax. This morning. From Ellis. It came through the fax machine at my work."

"Elizabeth, stop and think for a second. Could this be a hoax? Someone has to have that number and be playing with you."

"That's obviously the first thing I thought of too. But no one I know has the number to send a fax here! I didn't even know there WAS a fax machine here! I've been sitting here for an hour debating on whether or not I should even contact you. But, believe me when I say there isn't really a way that it could be a hoax from anyone. I know how crazy this must sound, but I promise you that I am not making this up. I would like to meet you for lunch if you are able. I'll bring the fax to give you and let you decide."

Calvin let out a long exhale. She sounded genuine but he struggled to figure out if it could possibly be real. Why would anyone make up something this bizarre in order to get him out to lunch? He made up his mind that it was worth taking it to the next step to see what this was all about. He also reminded himself that it was he who had taken the initiative with this woman to start the conversation and to bring up her dead friend.

"Okay, I can rearrange my schedule and meet you at noon. Let's say... Azteca on Main downtown?"

"Thank you Calvin," Elizabeth said softly, "I'll see you then."

He replayed the conversation in his mind. No matter how crazy it seemed, he sort of believed it.

The hours flew by as he had small fires to put out all morning. Before he knew it, it was ten minutes till noon. Walking out of his office, he called to his staff, "I'm going out to lunch; I'll be back soon. I have my cell if you guys need anything."

And just like that, he bounded down the stairwell toward the brisk outdoors and a lunch date with a *very* intriguing woman.

Calvin burst out the door at street level and had butterflies in his stomach to deal with in addition to the cold air. He couldn't help but be nervous. What kind of strange things were happening to him now? He entered the restaurant and looked around, spotting her quickly in the crowd of tables. She sat with a little girl who looked to be about five years old. The child had straight long brown hair and wore a pair of thick-lensed glasses that were perched precariously on the tip of her nose. She squinted down at the kids' menu coloring page, indicating her trouble seeing the menu clearly.

As he approached them, the girl's eyes beamed up at him through her glasses with an innocent gleam. Elizabeth quickly turned her head and nervously smiled at him.

"I am so glad you came. This is Grace."

"I am her nanny," she quickly added.

Calvin crouched to her level, reached over and took little Grace's hand to give it a soft shake in greeting. She beamed even more in delight with the special attention.

"It's nice to meet you Grace. That's a great picture you're coloring there."

As he sat down across from them, Elizabeth thrust a folded-in-half piece of paper in his direction, never looking up from her purse. She seemed determined in wasting no time with getting down to the task at hand.

He unfolded the slightly crumpled thin fax paper and read.

From:
To:
Subject:
Cities:

good morning Calvin
tell him thank you Elizabeth
you have a lot of work to do
he can help you find out
teach each other
use you spirit connections E train.
find him
no more pain
don't be afraid
congratulations on finding each other again
i miss you
i love you both
i would have approved and do
El

Calvin shuddered ever so slightly, yet uncontrollably, as shivers cascaded down his spinal column. He was so incredibly perplexed, confused and stunned that he didn't have any words to say after reading the fax except a mumbled, "Wow."

He sat and stared at it for a few more minutes, reading and re-reading it. Elizabeth let silence fill the air as the truth of the fax seeped in.

"Wow... but, I don't really understand what this means," he finally managed to say.

"If this is really from Ellis, why me? What does she mean when she says find him? What can he help you to find out?"

Elizabeth looked at him with caring eyes.

"I don't have all of the answers for you right now. I just know that this is from her though. She called me E Train, Calvin. It's a nickname that she had for me, and VERY few people ever even knew about it at all. It makes me believe unquestionably the authenticity of the source of this fax. I have no idea how she could even do that, but I am not questioning the fact that this is from my Ellis."

Her voice quivered and shook as the waiter came to take their order, forcing a much-needed pause in the conversation. Calvin's mind needed a moment to catch up. They ordered quickly and the waiter left. As his mind settled, he knew how he wanted to steer this conversation.

"Tell me about Ellis. I want to ask you a few questions about her if I can."

"Anything Calvin. It seems we're in this together, for whatever reason. Ask away."

"How did Ellis die?" he asked.

Elizabeth looked taken aback, yet quickly composed herself.

"She was murdered. She moved up to a small town in Canada with a man we hardly knew. She was out running one morning in a park. Someone attacked her and slit her throat," Elizabeth said as her eyes welled up with tears.

"And, as if that's not bad enough.... her body wasn't found for four days. They also found that she had been raped."

"Did they ever catch the guy?"

"They never found out who did it. It's an unsolved murder to this day. I had an uneasy feeling when she told me she was going to move up there. I should've stopped her, but I didn't. I feel so guilty over not being more vocal about it. But she had this new guy, she loved him, and that's what they wanted to do. I guess when a girl gets a man in her life, no matter how good her girlfriends are, she stops holding so much value in their opinions and listens more to what some guy wants than her best friend..." Elizabeth's voice trailed off as if remembering the conversation with Ellis.

Calvin nodded in understanding.

"I'm so sorry Elizabeth."

"One more thing," Elizabeth said, "She was pregnant when she was killed."

Calvin's eyes burned with tears as Elizabeth continued.

"That is partly why she married so suddenly and moved away to be with this guy. She didn't want to be a single mother, to try to raise a child alone... if she could prevent that by promising to move up north with him... he didn't want to stay in Spokane, so it was marry him and be up there, or be alone with their child here."

Calvin sat quietly for a moment as he collected his thoughts around the strange occurrences of the last six days. Why would Ellis's spirit want to find him? He never knew her or even Elizabeth for that matter. Was it her spirit compelling him to talk to Elizabeth in the first place? He didn't know where any of this was going and knew he just had to sit back and wait to see where the ride took him next. He figured if he started questioning things too much before he knew the facts, he would drive himself crazy with conjecture, and that wouldn't do anybody any good. Finally, he spoke.

"So, what do you make of this fax? What is she talking about with finding him? Are we supposed to try and solve her murder? Because I don't know if I am up for that. I mean, what am I supposed to do? Go to the police and tell them that I can communicate with this spirit who wants me to solve her murder that happened..." he paused, "When did it even happen?"

"Hold on a minute. I think that you are getting way ahead of yourself. I am not sure what Ellis wants us to do right now. It's true that her murder is unsolved. And it didn't happen that long ago. Her funeral was on April 28th of this year."

He shuddered again and suddenly felt chilled. Elizabeth looked at him imploringly, obviously noticing his shock. He replied in response to her quizzical look.

"April 28th is my birthday..."

"Wow," replied Elizabeth, "Mine is December 25."

It took a second to click in his mind, then he said, "Wow, a Christmas baby, huh?"

"Yes, the freakin' carpenter steals my birthday every year," she said.

He grinned, loving to hear another person speak with the same disregard to religion that he would. Plus, her remark provided a welcome laugh in an intense conversation.

Lunch arrived before he could even reply. He turned his attention to Grace.

"So Grace, how old are you?"

She looked shyly to Elizabeth, who nodded in an encouraging manner to put her shyness at ease. With this, the floodgates of five-year old banter opened completely.

"I am five years old. I go to Kindergarten, but not everyday. I have an older brother. He picks on me sometimes. Do you have a cat?"

Calvin laughed and nodded in the affirmative. "Yes, I do have a cat."

"What's its name? Is it a boy cat or a girl cat?"

"It's a girl cat, and her name is Mittens."

"Oh that's a pretty name. Like little gloves, right?"

"Yes, like little gloves," he replied to Grace.

They finished lunch with innocent conversation and laughs until it was time for Calvin to get back to work. With a quick kiss to Grace's little hand and a hug from Elizabeth, he was off and walking back to work.

He mused to himself how strange that conversation had been. He reached into his coat pocket and felt the fax paper that was folded up inside. Just touching it raised his heart rate.

"Christ... Maybe I shouldn't even tell Lisa about this one," he muttered to himself as he opened the door to the back stairwell that led up to his office.

Chapter 5
Honesty
Monday, November 28, 2005

"There's something that I need to show you from today."

"Okay, what is it? Something about work? Do you have a new script for me to read?"

Calvin often brought home copy from a new commercial he was working on to show Lisa.

"Not this time, actually it is a fax.... From Ellis."

In an effort to not keep secrets, Calvin had taken Lisa out to lunch the day after meeting Elizabeth to tell her about the experience of approaching the stranger and asking about her dead friend. Lisa, quick to write off such occurrences, took the news in stride but discounted the experience as coincidence.

Today's news didn't go over much better. Lisa's eyes opened wide in astonishment and she stood, dumbfounded. Calvin walked toward his coat that hung on a hook in the laundry room and pulled out the fax.

Lisa took it in her narrow, shaking hands. She read for what seemed like an eternity, obviously reading the message over and over.

"What does this mean? No way is this real. Why is she doing this to you Cal? Does she want help trying to solve her friend's murder? How did you even get this?"

"Slow down, I don't know what all of this means. And maybe I won't for a while. I don't know if I am supposed to find her murderer. God, I hope not. I was at work today when Elizabeth called and said that she got this fax at her work number."

"And you really believe that Calvin?" she asked. Her disapproving and emasculating tone had returned. "Well, honestly I didn't at first. But I met her for lunch, and after sitting and talking with her, I do believe it. She seemed as shocked and taken aback as I was about the whole fax thing. And she doesn't really seem to know what we are supposed to be doing for Ellis either. The bottom line is, I think that we just need to take this a day at a time and see how it all plays out."

"Calvin, it kind of scares me," said Lisa, "And I don't know what I can do about it. How can I trust this woman who obviously wants to spend time with you?"

"I know," he said, "It is a lot to handle. You know that I've NEVER believed in the thought of an afterlife, of God, of anything beyond this world. If anything's going to change my mind though, this would do it. At least about an afterlife. I still have my doubts about the whole God thing."

He continued, "I've told you about the strange things that used to happen to me. Maybe I was so opposed to spirits because I have been trying to deny it all these years. I always thought religion or belief in any afterlife was a sign of weakness; something people made up to help them deal with the unknown. I'm not weak, and I've never needed that 'made up' reassurance that there is anything after death. Plus, shit Lisa, I haven't had anything weird happen since The Night of Pitchfork Man. And that was ten years ago."

Chapter 6
The Night of Pitchfork Man
Friday, June 2, 1995

It was a beautiful late spring evening.
After spending their date night at a park on the
shores of the Spokane River, Calvin and Lisa, both
just 18 years old, drove to the expansive and deserted
parking lot of a high school football stadium. The
stadium, close to Lisa's house, was the perfect place
to pass the time before getting her home, just
seconds before her midnight curfew.
    They spent most of the time talking and
listening to music on the radio.
"I love you. I can see us spending our lives together
Calvin," Lisa said.
Calvin didn't reply. He felt distracted by something
he couldn't see. Something didn't feel right, but he
couldn't tell what. A wave of fear grew in him and his
heart rate picked up. He broke out in a cold sweat.
"What's wrong? I didn't mean I want us to get
married right now... I was just..."
"That's not it Lisa. We've got to get out of here," he
said as he quickly put on his seat belt, looking
straight out the front window as if something should
be there. He searched for something to explain the
fear... a cop, her dad... something. He saw nothing.
"What?" Lisa asked. "Is it almost midnight already?"
"Lisa, we have to get out of here right now," he said
as he started the car and spun the tires in the gravel
parking lot, desperate to leave. Calvin was visibly
spooked, and at what he had no idea.
"Calvin, what's the matter!?"
"I don't know. But we have to leave here. Right now!"

There was urgency in his voice that even he had never heard before.

Calvin remained intent on driving and didn't pause to give Lisa the reassuring smile he normally would in a stressful situation. This time he knew something was wrong. He felt something pressed in around them, like something was approaching but from EVERYWHERE. He knew that if he didn't speed out of there now, something terrible would happen. Staying in place would only tempt disaster and that wasn't an option.

Not today.

"Well, where are you going? This isn't the way to my house..."

"I don't know where I'm going," he said urgently, pressing on the gas.

Calvin remained quiet, concentrating on something he knew Lisa couldn't feel or understand. He took a sudden right turn onto Post Street.

"Why are you turning here? It's just residential...you aren't acting like yourself!"

He didn't answer because he didn't know.

Then he saw the man.

"Did you see that guy?" Calvin asked, his voice shooting through the silence.

"No, what guy? Where? What did he look like?"

"That guy. He stood on the corner back there, under the tree. He was holding a pitchfork..."

The man had long scraggly hair, piercing dark eyes, unkempt facial hair, and torn clothes. He didn't appear to belong in a middle-class neighborhood; especially near midnight.

After passing the man, Calvin furtively glanced in his rearview mirror and could still see the man's eyes following his car along with the tines of the pitchfork reflecting in the red of his Honda's tail lights.

Calvin made a hard right turn.

"What has gotten into you? Where are you going?"

Lisa trembled in fear.

"I'm going back to look at him again. I can't believe you didn't see him! He was so tall..."

Calvin's voice drifted off as he pictured the man in his mind.

"He was right on the corner underneath a big tree, he was shadowed but I saw his long black hair, a long beard, and his eyes... they stared right into the car and followed us," he said, turning onto Post again.

Lisa peered through the darkness.

Calvin slowed the car as he approached the corner where Pitchfork Man stood.

This time the corner sat empty.

"Calvin, really...a man with a pitchfork? At this hour? You know how crazy that sounds?"

Lisa's cynical and analytical tone crept into her voice. "Really, what would a man with a pitchfork be doing standing underneath a tree on Post Street at midnight?! Grow a brain."

"Lisa," he said her name in exasperation, "I know what I saw."

He turned onto the arterial heading back toward Lisa's house. A street light burned out above the car. It wasn't the first time he'd noticed that happen, but that night was the first time he really paid attention to it. He wasn't sure if Lisa had noticed.

They were both quiet as he drove, processing the strange events that had just taken place. Lisa's tight lips and crossed arms showed her disturbed disapproval as they arrived back at her house.

The end of their date had been so bizarre that it put a strange feel on their entire afternoon and evening together. Lisa remained silent. Turning the ignition off, Calvin leaned over to give her a hug, which Lisa resisted at first.

He took a deep breath and felt better for a moment. Calvin looked out the rear passenger-side window as they embraced, and saw it slowly fog up.

Calvin's heart leapt into high speed again as the temperature in the car dropped drastically. No other windows fogged over. He raised his eyes to glance out the back passenger window again.

His eyes widened in surprise. Lisa lifted her head too and looked toward the back of the car.

Neither spoke as they watched an image slowly form; like someone drawing on the rear window from inside the car.

A flood of adrenaline coursed through his body. Right before their eyes was a picture of a cross-like dagger, drawn in the mist on the window.

"Oh my God!" Lisa exclaimed, terrified and paralyzed in fear. Calvin put a hand on her shoulder and she yelped, but it was enough to encourage her to exit and get as much space between herself and that car as possible.

They ran to the front porch and with a quick kiss on the cheek Calvin sent her inside.

Then he turned back toward the car. Not too keen to climb back into it, he knew he didn't have a choice and slowly approached. With a glance into the back seat to make absolutely sure that it remained empty, he opened the door and collapsed inside.

He knew logically that there wasn't anything in the back seat, but he could feel something there. There was an undeniable presence, powerful and overpowering, behind him as he drove.

He put on his signal to take a right onto Lowell Street and head home.

"NO!"

The booming male voice seemed to come from all around, and made him jump in his seat. While the voice was loud and strong, it felt more protective than threatening. He didn't question it and continued without taking the turn. After a few blocks he glanced down Barnes Road, which was bathed in light. Although puzzled, he took this as a sign that it was okay to turn, and he did. Two more turns and he pulled safely into the driveway at his parents' house.

Calvin hurriedly entered the code to open the garage door then made his way through the compact space between his dad's car and the bicycles hanging on the wall, careful to avoid contact with them. He reached the door that led into the house, grabbed the doorknob, took a deep breath, and hesitantly looked back, hoping he wouldn't see anything but terrified that he would.

The pedals of the bikes rotated, first on the bicycle farthest from him, then on the nearest, as though someone following him had bumped the pedals that he so carefully avoided. He threw open the door, turned to take one last look at whatever was behind him, and felt a rush of penetrating cold pass through the very core of his body. He slammed the door and ran down the stairs to his room, jumping into his bed, shivering from the combination of cold and fear.

"Go away go away go away go away," he chanted, panicked and curled up under his covers. "Whatever you are, leave me alone. I give up, just go away… forever."

Calvin lay in his bed, light on, trying to recover and let his body calm down enough to get some sleep. He could still feel the adrenaline, and his mind raced as he replayed the events of the night over and over, trying to figure out what it could all mean. All he knew for sure was that for the first time in his life, and hopefully the last, he felt pure evil.

This was *nothing* like the innocent experiences that began when he was a child. He racked his brain looking for some sign of evil in the things he used to see. He remembered the glowing orbs hanging in his room and at the base of the stairs, the magazine pages fluttering on his dresser… things that were enough to keep him up at night as a child, but not even remotely as scary as tonight's occurrences.

He pulled the covers tighter around him and fell asleep to those thoughts. Calvin didn't wake until morning and felt fuzzy and disoriented, like the previous evening's occurrences had been a horrific nightmare.

Thirsty, he walked upstairs and into the kitchen and opened the door of the refrigerator to get some juice. His mom stood near the kitchen table wearing her robe and glasses.

"Calvin!" she exclaimed. "What on earth happened to your back?"

"What?" he asked, surprised.

He rushed into the laundry room where a mirror hung above the sink. His eyes widened in astonishment as he looked over his shoulder. Extending from his collarbones, over his shoulders and down the length of his back were eight bright red, inflamed scratches, still sticky with blood that hadn't fully dried.

...

November 28, 2005

"What if this is related somehow, Lisa?" Calvin asked, holding up the fax.

"What if I've been shoving some kind of spiritual ability under the surface since I was a child? What if now there is a strong and determined enough spirit, one that won't be denied the help that I can somehow offer?"

"You don't even believe in the afterlife Calvin. These have to be coincidences. Seriously, think," Lisa replied.

"And what about Sterling's dreams?" Cal continued, ignoring his wife's snide comment.

"Our son has been waking up almost every night convinced that a scary man with sharp blue teeth tickles his back and scoops him up in a pillowcase to take him away. The kid won't even sleep with a pillowcase anymore. Something's going on here."

"I think you're wrong," she said, "And I hope you let this craziness go soon."

"I wish I could. You remember Pitchfork Man. That was over within a couple of hours. Somehow I don't feel like this is going away as easily this time..."

Chapter 7
Seeing Ellis
Tuesday, December 6th, 2005

Calvin glanced at his watch.
4:33.
Normally he could leave the office by 4:00, so he knew he'd better call Lisa to let her know there would be an empty seat for dinner tonight.

He felt like it was going to be another very long evening but all he wanted was to go home, crawl into bed, and sleep.

The emotional turmoil of the previous week already had taken a toll. The more he tried to think about it and make sense of it all, the more it drained his energy. He did his best to keep it on the back burner and even pretend that it wasn't really happening, just like he'd done with spiritual events his entire life. Maybe the commercial shoot and meeting Elizabeth, the strange visions, and the fax were all just pieces of a strange and sustained reality; a series of events explainable by coincidence and science, if only he was alert enough to think clearly. He halfway wondered if he had fallen asleep while watching TV in bed and had somehow created an entirely parallel stream of consciousness based on something he saw. He seriously wondered if he was going insane, and that scared him. The lack of support from Lisa certainly wasn't helping his emotional state.

Calvin felt that this new spiritual stress, combined with all of the stress that was just typical in his day-to-day job was too much. He thought for just a moment that it might be wise to pursue some counseling.

That would sure freak Lisa out, he thought.

He couldn't really imagine going home and telling her that he thought he needed to see a counselor. He didn't want to see the look in her eyes. He knew her well; it would be a look of worry, of judgment.

He knew that his boss had gone to counseling for a while to deal with work stress and a failing marriage. He thought maybe he'd ask for a name and just keep it to himself.

With that, he affirmed to himself that when he got the chance, he would ask Casey for the name of a counselor and see if he could arrange the appointments to occur during the lunch hour. Then maybe an impartial third party could tell him if he was losing his mind or not.

The brief conversation with himself made him feel just a little better; somehow slightly more energized and ready to face what may come in the evening stretching before him. He didn't feel quite so tired or crazy, just by considering the possibility of a counselor.

After all, crazy people don't take themselves to counseling, so he figured he must still have a logical mind.

He picked up the phone to call Lisa since another ten minutes had slipped by since he first thought to call her. He braced himself for the argument against being late again. He never knew how Lisa was going to answer the phone these days. It was completely dependent on her day at work, and how well the children were playing together.

The phone only rang twice before Lisa answered with a frazzled, "Hello?"

"Hey. I won't make it home for dinner tonight. We have a commercial shoot downtown, and it doesn't start until six. By the time I could make it home, I would have to turn around and drive right back to the shoot."

He spoke quickly so he could get it all out in one big sentence so that Lisa wouldn't interrupt him with a complaint before he had given his full excuse.

Lisa let out an exasperated sigh.

"Well Cal, it would've been nice if you could've picked up the phone to call me BEFORE you were supposed to already be home!"

Lisa's voice cracked as she spoke.

"Is it really that hard to pick up the damn phone when it is sitting six inches from your hand to call me BEFORE I have the dinner out and dished up? You don't seem to realize that I work so hard to make a nice meal and create a loving family dinner atmosphere, and when you do this to me, you basically dismiss all my efforts. I don't know why I even bother cooking anymore. I give up!"

"Sorry, I didn't know that I had to call you by a certain time. It was a busy, hard day for me too Lisa. At least I called!"

"Calvin, don't get all pissy with me! You don't know what it's like!"

She composed herself and, on the verge of tears quietly said, "Do you even realize how much I anticipate you coming home?"

"Stop smothering me, please. I am your husband, not your kid. There isn't a time when I even have to be home. I don't have a curfew. I have to work late so give me a break. I just wanted to call you and let you know, not get lectured about it."

"You know Calvin," Lisa said through tears, "You are doing it again. Just like you have with every other job you have had since we have been married. You have NO BALANCE in your life anymore. Your work is consuming you. You lack common courtesy for me. All you care about is your commercials. Well, what about me? What about my sanity? My work day? Do you even care about that? I have been telling you how crappy I have been feeling for months now. And it takes some dead woman to talk to you to open up a part of you that I can't get to. Good luck tonight! I guess I'll see you when I see you!"

He heard a muffled goodbye as Lisa quickly hung up the phone, not giving him time to respond to her tirade.

His face flushed in anger. He thought that she was completely overreacting yet again.

God, I'm living with my mother....

He closed his laptop and turned to the back of his chair where his jacket hung. As he glanced up toward the door, he saw the outline of a figure looming; floating. It was just from the corner of his eye, but definitely a woman with long brown hair. His adrenaline soared and he whipped his head in her direction to get a closer look, but she was gone. Even though it was quick, he could tell the figure was a human form, though completely iridescent.

Ellis?

With adrenaline still pumping, he could feel the fear and excitement all at once.

She disappeared almost as soon as he noticed her. He blinked several times, hoping to will her back into the room. It was so fast. Her form was noticeable out of the corner of his eye, but when he stopped to focus on it, to really look, she disappeared.

He knew that people quickly discount or write off visions like this, attributing them to a fallacy of the mind. It is human nature to always doubt. He doubted visions like this his whole life, but now it felt different. In the past he would have attributed this to an overactive imagination, but combined with the events of meeting Elizabeth and receiving the fax, he now felt open to this being a glimpse into something deeper than the here and now. What was once such a resolute wall toward anything other than the current life, he was now heading down the path of becoming less skeptical about the existence of life after death. He reached for his jacket yet again, and headed out of the office to go to the shoot.

It was a short distance through downtown so Calvin walked, hoping the cool crisp air would clear his mind. He headed down the familiar stairwell and tonight could have sworn that he heard laughter coming from somewhere behind the concrete walls. He smiled as he pushed open the door and was greeted with the autumn evening.

The air was a cool and refreshing change from the stuffiness that he felt in his office. The shoot location, only 10 minutes away on foot, was inside an old power-generation building that had been renovated into offices, a restaurant, and a bar. He expected everything to go fairly smoothly tonight since the script was simple and actors were experienced.

The building fascinated him. The film production company he worked with had their offices here as well, and the owner had told him a few ghost stories. Oddly enough, the more he paid attention and didn't discount others' stories as moronic, the more he realized that people all around him had seen, heard, or felt things before too. He had always just assumed they were wrong or not educated enough to know the truth.

When he arrived, the production people already had the lighting set up. There were only two actors, and they were both ready when he walked in. This is how he liked it to be done. All Calvin had to do was direct the actors on how to speak their lines and not have to worry about lighting and other details.

The bar in the basement of the building had a Gonzaga Bulldogs basketball game on and he wanted to monitor that as he simultaneously kept tabs on the shoot.

The shoot did indeed go as smoothly as he'd hoped and when they finished, the game was in its final minutes. Not being in a hurry to go home after the argument with Lisa, Calvin headed down to the bar to watch the rest of the game. He knew the kids would already be in their bedtime routine, and even if he went home now, he was going to miss seeing them awake anyway.

A couple of others from the shoot joined him, and they found seats up at the counter within view of the screen to watch the game.

He cheered as the Bulldogs scored another two points, picked up a beer and took a deep swig.

Out of the corner of his eye, to his left and back in the corner of the bar, he was surprised to see a pretty blonde. He instinctively did a double take.

His eyes met Elizabeth's, who sat with a group of women. She smiled at him, and he nodded in acknowledgement and recognition. He couldn't believe it, and his heart beat faster with excitement as he looked at her.

"Hey guys, I just saw a friend over there. I'm going to go see her, I'll see ya later," he said as he started to make his way toward her.

"Elizabeth, I can't believe it! How's it going?" he asked as he approached.

She quickly moved some things over on the table and motioned to an empty chair.

"So very nice to see you Calvin, what a surprise! These are some friends of mine, Cindy, Veronica, and Georgia. We're out just having some girl time, away from our husbands. Girls, this is my friend Calvin."

They exchanged hellos and hand shakes as he settled down next to Elizabeth.

The other girls resumed their conversation, which created a nice distraction for Elizabeth and Calvin to talk relatively unnoticed.

At one point they found themselves not even talking, just looking into each other's eyes.

That's when she said, "You saw her, didn't you?"

Calvin was surprised, but not shocked, as he nodded, smiled, and answered, "Yeah, I did... how'd you know that?"

"I just do. Where did you see her? Tell me about it," she said, almost demanding but in the sweetest way he could imagine. She leaned forward, put her elbows on the table and her hands under her chin, like what he was about to say was her only interest in the world.

"Well, I was in my office, going to reach for my coat to come here for a shoot. And out of the corner of my eye, I saw the form of a woman…"

Elizabeth nodded in understanding.

"I had a feeling that it wouldn't be long before you would be able to see things. You are progressing quickly. You must have a unique office… not a lot of disruption to the energy flow…"

He took this as a question as to whether she could see his office or not. Answering her before she had a chance to fully ask, "I could show you my office if you want…"

Elizabeth didn't need any time to think about it. She turned to her friends and said, "Ladies, I am gonna head out with Calvin, I'll see you all later okay?"

She gave the women hugs and turned to walk out the door.

The walk to the office was quick, and they spoke very little on the way. Calvin's heart raced as he realized he was going to be alone in his office with the woman from the shoot. The feeling was a little odd, as they hadn't known each other for very long, and he could feel that there was already an attraction developing. There was an intense connection that was almost too strange to be believable.

Elizabeth paused as they made their way up the back stairwell. Standing about a third of the way up the first staircase, she looked at something. She smiled, and glanced over to Calvin.

"Can you see her?" she whispered.

Calvin looked in front of him first, and then behind. "See who?"

"That woman who just passed us," Elizabeth said, giggling, "She was dressed like a flapper and drunk out of her mind. She was laughing and stumbling down the stairs."

She turned to him, quite delighted and said, "Does this stairwell ever feel strange to you?"

Once again, he was amazed by this unbelievable and intoxicating woman. Maybe there was something to the laughter he heard after all. He'd heard stories that the building used to house a basement speakeasy in the 1920s. The laughter he'd heard was probably the drunken laughter of some of the old customers who frequented here in their lifetime.

"Whoa. Just tonight, in fact, I came down here and thought that I heard laughing."

"Calvin, you really need to learn to just slow down, stop, and feel things. Trust your intuition, you'll find it's usually right. You have to just stop questioning yourself long enough to let go of any preconceived notions that you have built up. You'll learn. You still have a long way to go."

He chose not to ask for details on that comment, as they only had a short distance left to climb. Turning left at the top of the stairwell, they faced the entrance to his darkened office. He reached into his pocket and pulled out the door key.

"This is it," he said as he unlocked the door and swung it open.

Elizabeth followed him inside to the lobby. The office suite was quiet and dark, except for the soft glow from the office Christmas tree that they'd put up shortly after Thanksgiving. Neither of them reached for the light switch, knowing that turning on the overhead fluorescents would kill the moment. Instead they just stood in the silence and felt the energy around them while appreciating the quiet. Calvin walked in the dark toward the open door of his corner office and Elizabeth followed with smooth gliding steps and a knowing smirk on her face.

"This is where I saw her," he said, gesturing toward the doorway and off to the right side of his desk. Elizabeth nodded as she glanced around and said in a near whisper, "You really have the perfect place to sit and let them come to you. Just try to keep the lights off, and don't look for them. When you see something out of the corner of your eye, try to resist looking directly at it, or it will disappear."

He felt lost. This was all so incredibly foreign to him. He glanced down at his watch and saw that it was already past ten o' clock and he knew that he had better be getting home.

He looked back toward the Christmas tree, and then couldn't look away. Elizabeth stared at it too and he knew she saw the same things he did. Dark shadows passed in front of the individual lights on the tree, temporarily blocking their light and creating an eerie twinkling effect.

He uttered a "Wow..."

"See Cal," Elizabeth said in a whisper, "They are here. Always here. Always around you. Always watching. Can you feel the cold?"

"Where?" he asked.

"Just put out your hands, and... feel. You'll feel cold patches," said Elizabeth.

He extended his hands out in front of him, slowly moving them from right to left, then right again. Elizabeth gently placed a hand on his and guided him, his pulse quickened at her touch.

"Right here. I feel it," he said.

"Yes, that's them," replied Elizabeth with a quiet excitement.

They stood there silent, her hand still wrapped around his and their eyes locking. Her scent permeated his soul and he felt an incredible peace. And then guilt.

He nervously glanced away for a moment, toward the door and gasped.

"Elizabeth, look at my office door," he said, noticing the glass pane beginning to fog up.

She let out a soft chuckle and leaned in close to him, their shoulders now touching.

She whispered into his ear, "You noticed... that's another sign. That's the kind of thing you need to be open to and watch for. Isn't it... magical? Subtle, yes, but magical when your eyes are open to it."

"It's amazing," he said, his voice drifting as he lost himself in the flickering of the lights and the fogged window.

The fogged window. He snapped out of this incredible moment by the memory of the fogged window in his car on the night of Pitchfork Man. Elizabeth let go of his hand.

"I'm sure that this will all take me some time to get used to. I am trying... but I haven't had much time to digest or make sense of this whole thing. I really need to get home or my wife will be worried."

He walked toward the door, and Elizabeth followed. "I should get home to my husband too."

"So you're married too?"

"Yes, five years. Seems like we have a lot in common! I know that this all seems so weird to you right now. But Calvin, you can't really imagine how wonderful it is for me to finally have someone else who can see these things, who can do what I can do. In time, you will understand more of your abilities, and I can help you learn how to use them."

She reached for his upper arm, lightly touching him to make him turn to look at her. She leaned into him again and softly said, "Really, it is both a blessing and a curse. But I will help you to understand, in any way that I can. After all, I have been doing this since I was three, and looking for you for nearly as long..."

He nodded and looked at her with a confused look on his face and began to walk, slowly, toward the door.

"I just don't understand what it is that Ellis wants from us."

Elizabeth replied, "I don't either Cal, but I have a feeling that it won't take us very long to find out."

Chapter 8
Sparkle Guy
Friday, December 9, 2005

'Calvin,' the email began, *'The girl I nanny for, Grace, told me she wanted to tell the "Sparkle Guy" something... She calls you that because she said you had sparkles all around you when she saw you. Anyway, I just had to email this to you, I wrote it the way she said it so you could imagine her cute little voice. Here it is...*
Seeing Elizabeth's name in his email had yet to lead to disappointment. Even in the midst of another busy day at work, Calvin continued reading her message, intrigued.
"Well...you know...it's cold where you are sometimes? Well, that girl...she says you keep her warm...it was cold where she was and she can't, you know, get warm always... Elizabeth, is he going to be mad at me for saying this stuff? It's embarrassing."
Puzzled, Calvin sat for a moment, re-reading the message. Then another email popped into the inbox. He quickly opened it.
"Cal, I didn't know Grace was like this... I'm dumbfounded. I'm guessing that when she met you, there was a connection formed, and Ellis was able to send her what she needed to say. Here's some more, exactly as she said it:
"You know... I have somefin else to tell ya... it's special peacause... well, now I'm really embarrassed. But that girl had a baby in her tummy you know... and somefin else..."
"She's tryin to talk to you, ya know."
"Listen to me peacause I can tell you what she wants to say right now."

46

"She says that she doesn't, well, she doesn't really know the man in the park. She can't tell me about the park, well peacause I'm a kiddo."
"She was a runner girl."
"And she was running peacause Paul and her had a fight."
"And the next thing she knows she can't breathe so very good."
"And then it went dark."
"She says it didn't hurt. She must be thinking about her legs from running peacause that's all I can guess."
"She says you can't find the man in the park. You're not 'posed to. But that she can rest now 'cause you're gonna help more people in this life. She says you heard her whisper that day. And to be careful peacause it's a real thing."
"And one more thing. She kinda, sorta, wants to know if she can protect that little girl who lives with you. She misses her little girl."

Calvin was absolutely and totally, in Elizabeth's words, dumbstruck. He couldn't even formulate an answer for Elizabeth on those emails right away. He printed them, folded up the papers, and put them in his pocket. He logged off the computer and stood up to leave, grabbing his jacket and quickly making his way out the door.

He was in such a haze after that he barely even registered the drive to pick up Sterling and Hannah, his kids. Upon arriving at Donna's house, their daycare lady, both kids were happy and ready to come home. They happily bounced out the door and ambled to the car.

The house felt dark and empty upon arrival. Calvin flipped on a couple of lamps and hit the switch to ignite the home's gas fireplace, hoping to bring some light into the cold home.

A warm glow on the porch from the hanging pendent light welcomed Lisa home shortly after. Calvin hoped it was all enough light to counteract the news of the emails.

"Hey," he said, greeting her as she came in the garage door with an armful of mail.

"Mommy!" Sterling cried.

"Mommy!" Hannah replicated, in her sweet 18-month old voice.

"Hi my babies," Lisa said with a smile as she crouched down to child height, still in the doorway from the laundry room, which connected the great room to the garage.

"Hey Cal," Lisa said, "How was your day?"

"Uh, you know. It went well," he said, "A little weird though actually. I have something to show you."

"What is it?"

He retrieved the printed emails from his pocket and headed back toward the granite-slathered kitchen island where they had gathered to talk.

"This is an email that I got today at work. Just read it," he said.

Lisa reached out her hand to take the papers. Calvin noticed that her hands shook ever so slightly as she read. She finished, looked up, and said, "Wow..." in a barely audible whisper.

"I know," Calvin replied.

"You know Elizabeth could have just written all of this," Lisa said, in her defiant tone.

"Seriously? This is the first time I've ever even slightly believed anything like this, and you won't support me?"

"And support this woman trying to swoop in on my husband? Even if it is true, it says you don't have to find her killer right?"

"It doesn't look like it...."

"So you're going to believe that, for some reason, this dead girl had to get you and Elizabeth together. Grace even says that Ellis... 'Can rest because you're gonna help more people in this life... ' What exactly do you think that means?"

"I don't know. This is all just so crazy. How am I supposed to help people? And why did she lead me to Elizabeth? It seems weird," he said as he shook his head slowly. He was still trying to digest it all as much as Lisa was trying to accept it.

To Calvin, it seemed as though he and Elizabeth needed to be in contact with each other for reasons still unknown. Maybe she could help him to realize the full potential of his abilities and put them to good use. Maybe he could help people by answering the seemingly unanswerable questions from beyond the grave.

As soon as he even had the thought, he pushed it away as an absurd notion. After all, before any of these communications with Ellis, he didn't even believe that there *was* anything beyond the grave.

Calvin was a pretty hard-core atheist. He'd been baptized Catholic but certainly wouldn't have had he any choice in the matter. He spent the majority of his 28 years feeling like he'd burst into flames even just passing a church. On the rare occasions he had to enter one, his blood boiled with anger and complete disbelief that people believed the stories told inside the walls. Since he was a child he believed that organized religion was a brain-washing, fear-based propaganda machine that only served to comfort the weak.

Choosing not to believe eventually took away Calvin's fear of the dark and gave him many nights of peaceful sleep.

His refusal to attend church put an end to Lisa's semi-regular attendance, though she never doubted the existence of God. They often debated the topic but sat on opposite sides of the religious fence.

Before meeting Elizabeth, the occurrence with Pitchfork Man and the mysterious orbs in his basement bedroom were not enough to convince him that anything existed beyond the tangible world. Although he remembered each event in detail, he fully believed that it was something that science would one day be able to explain.

This time though, there was too much going on. There were too many coincidences to foster his denial and it began to change the entire relativity of his world. He was no longer in denial, but had moved to a state of shock.

"Calvin!"

Lisa's voice broke him out of his reverie.

"Sorry, I was just thinking about all of this," he said slowly, "It is so much to digest. It's seriously turned things up-side-down for me. I guess we'll just have to take this day by day, and see where it leads. I think that there seems to be a purpose that we don't know about yet, and I don't think that we are at the point of figuring that out. It's just something that will probably play itself out."

"Yes, I'm sure you're right. Either that or you're going batshit crazy."

Cal wondered how much more of this she could take before labeling him as a mental patient freak.

He needed a second opinion. He called his parents, the people who never once judged him for the spiritual things that happened in the basement as a child.

After the kids and his wife went to bed, Rick and Kelli Janek knocked softly on the front door.

His mom sat on the floor next to the armchair where his dad had settled. They both had concerned looks on their faces, wondering why their son would ask them to come over so late in the evening.

"Well, I guess I'll just get right to it," he said nervously. He knew his parents would not question him, but the thought of talking about the events made him feel like maybe it was all nothing more than a series of coincidences. He was especially nervous about his dad's reaction, as they'd always shared views on religion and the afterlife. Regardless, he kept talking.

"Okay, you know how, when I was a kid, I'd tell you about the orbs of light I'd see, and the other crazy stuff that would happen to me? Mom, remember telling me to look for the light before I'd go to sleep so I wouldn't be afraid, and when I told you about seeing the man with the pitchfork?"

His parents both nodded.

"Well, apparently that was all real. And the spirits are back. Kind of with a vengeance, actually..."

He proceeded to tell them everything; from the night he met Elizabeth to the connection to Ellis. He handed them the fax and the printed emails from Elizabeth.

Dad wiped away a tear as he finished reading, and uttered a barely audible, "Wow."

Mom smiled at him with watery eyes.

"So that's all the information I have right now. I don't know why any of this is happening, but I wanted to tell you," he said.

"You trust her, this Elizabeth?" Dad said, his skepticism beginning to show through.

"I think so Dad, this is just too big of a coincidence to be faked. And really, why would a stranger go through all this just to pull a hoax on me? That wouldn't make sense."

Dad nodded and Mom smiled.

"Just be careful, Calvin, and stay in the light, okay? I've always known you were special," Mom said.

Mom often talked about 'the light' and her spiritual side, which Calvin wrote off as new-age freako shit. This time he just smiled and nodded.

"Well, I have to work tomorrow," said his dad as he looked at his watch, "We better get going. Keep us updated. I'm proud of you, and I believe you."

"Thanks Dad, that means a lot. I love you. Thanks for coming up tonight," he said.

Just before Calvin crawled into bed, Sterling's frightened voice broke the silence.

"Daaaaaady! Mommy? DADDY!"

Calvin rushed to his son.

Tears streamed down Sterling's face. He looked terrified.

"Oh, buddy! What is it?" He worriedly inquired as he scooped the child into his arms.

"The man.... With the sharp blue teeth!" he cried.

"Oh kiddo...It's just a bad dream. There is no man with blue teeth here."

He tried to be comforting, yet at the same time his room felt uncomfortable cold. Calvin knew this had to be more than a bad dream.

"He was here. The hands... they were tickling my back again," he said, his tiny voice quivering.

Calvin kissed his head and held him tight to his heart, attempting to fill his son with love.

Eventually he settled down and laid his head back on his pillow, sans pillowcase. Exhausted, his breathing soon became deeper and rhythmic.

As Calvin stood to leave, he saw that Lisa had been standing in the doorway, watching them silently.

Calvin closed the door behind him, and his wife said, "I just don't know what to do about these nightmares Cal. It stresses him out. And they are always the same. Those hands. And the man with the blue teeth, it gives me the creeps."

"Just bad dreams, I'm sure," Calvin lied.

"Let's go to bed."

Chapter 9

Contact

Wednesday, December 14th, 2005

The kids were a refreshing sight after a grueling day at work.

At Donna's house, Sterling and Hannah both scampered off their bar stools and ran into Calvin's arms, both squealing, "Daddy!"

He hugged them both at the same time, relishing the feeling of their heads nuzzled into his chest and inhaling the soft scent of their hair. He smiled. When he felt so physically exhausted and mentally drained after work, his children were vibrant balls of uplifting energy and his biggest source of much-needed light.

"Let's go home guys," he said as he helped them put on their boots, coats, hats, and gloves.

He kept the radio off as they drove the short distance up the windy dirt road to their house. He wanted to give them time to sit and relax in some peaceful quiet before the bustle of the transition to home, getting dinner, and playing began.

After entering the house, Calvin switched on the computer, figuring he should have enough time to chat with Elizabeth for a few minutes and then throw something on the stove for dinner before Lisa walked in the door.

Just as he had hoped, he saw Elizabeth online. His heart quickened its pace in anticipation of what might unfold.

The screen name she used got his attention quickly, as it happened to be a phrase from one of his children's favorite bedtime books. He double clicked on her name and sent a message.

CALVIN says:

Hi Elizabeth, are you there?

To the moon...and back says:
Is this Calvin?

He was slightly taken aback, as that question told him the person responding was obviously not Elizabeth. He simply typed.

CALVIN says:
Yup.

To the moon...and back says:
It's Jack

His pulse quickened and his heart sank as he wondered what Elizabeth's husband thought of him wanting to chat with his wife.
Another message blipped on the screen.

To the moon...and back says:
I don't know how to say this to you
But Elizabeth may need a minute

CALVIN says:
Alright... Good meeting you.

To the moon...and back says:
I will probably leave her alone.
I don't like seeing her like this
When you're done chatting just wait...
She eventually snaps back

Snaps back? Back from what?

He felt anxious and scared, wishing he'd never even logged on. Maybe if Jack could snap Elizabeth out of whatever state she was in...

CALVIN says:
Can you try to snap her out of it for me?

To the moon...and back says:
I can try if this makes you uncomfortable.
We can talk about this when we meet if you want

He had forgotten that he spoke with Elizabeth about getting the two couples together to meet. He made a mental note to mention it to Lisa.

CALVIN says:
I know my wife will want to talk to you.

To the moon...and back says:
From my experience when it happens, it just happens.
She has no clue she's not here.
She'll be disoriented when she comes back.

Calvin was pretty damn disoriented himself at this point and didn't know what Jack was talking about. He kept his cool and just kept typing.

CALVIN says:
Jack- thanks for being so cool about this. This is a weird situation for me!

To the moon...and back says:

Hey man, I've been there. Look who I live with.
And whatever you want her to know after this chat,
you'll have to remind her of.
I'll explain when we meet. I have sympathy for your
wife if you are anything like mine.
I'll leave you two alone to chat.
This really zaps Elizabeth though.
One warning:
Be careful what you ask, you might learn things you
shouldn't.
Give her a couple minutes.
Bye.

CALVIN says:
bye man

He sat silent... heart pounding in anticipation,
wondering what was about to happen. What was
Elizabeth doing on her side of the computer? Could
this all be a hoax?
He stared at the screen, re-reading what Jack had
said. His logical mind asked why in the world a
strange woman AND her husband would conspire
against him to make him think he's crazy. This just
didn't feel like a joke. He took slow, heavy breaths as
he watched the screen.
Then it blipped again.

To the moon...and back says:
keep breathing

CALVIN says:
Elizabeth?

To the moon...and back says:
She'll be back in a moment.
But I have not left

He was confused. If this WAS Elizabeth, why did she just say that? He sat, wrapping his arms around himself as he shivered, wishing he switched on the gas fireplace when he got home. He waited for more words to come across.

To the moon...and back says:
The cold you feel is natural.
I trust her with you.
Rearrange the children's rooms,
Their sleep will be more sound

Calvin's mind exploded in silent thought as he questioned how anyone could know about the problems sleeping.

To the moon...and back says:
Why do you question me?

That got his attention. Somehow whoever this was could hear his thoughts. He leaned in toward the monitor, his eyes glued to the screen in front of him...still in a state of disbelief and wonder.

To the moon...and back says:
You're wondering if I can hear you

Holy shit.

To the moon...and back says:

You wonder if 'They' can hear you
We always have
You just stopped listening.
The feeling you have right now...
The wave of energy
The dizziness
The cold
The ache between your ear and jaw you get
sometimes
The tightness in your lower back
And the stomach grumbles
All signs we are near

These were all symptoms he'd experienced... reading them here rendered him nearly speechless. He managed to type the only words he could think to ask:

CALVIN says:
Who are you?

To the moon...and back says:
To you? Or to e-train?

With that, Calvin knew with whom he was speaking.

To the moon...and back says:
I'm a messenger
And a friend

CALVIN says:
What do you need from me? Can I help you?

To the moon...and back says:

You have helped me.
And you did hear me before the child, Grace, did.
I've been trying for nearly four months.

And in a sudden realization of shock, amazement and damn near disbelief, it fully clicked. His eyes welled up with tears as he typed.

CALVIN says:
Oh my God...Ellis...

To the moon...and back says:
You can recall the time.

CALVIN says:
When?

To the moon...and back says:
You tell me when you first heard me say 'stop,' and you stopped.
Mid walk
Four months ago

He remembered...

CALVIN says:
On the stairs....

On that day, Calvin needed to go downstairs to grab some items out of storage, but distinctly remembered hearing someone tell him to stop before he reached the basement. He thought it was Lisa before remembering he was home alone.

To the moon...and back says:
Yes. Calvin, I never believed Elizabeth when I was alive
I took her as a novelty.
She knew things no one could,
Yet I couldn't believe.

CALVIN says:
And that's how you helped me... To believe. I have to believe now. Thank you.

To the moon...and back says:
Why are you thanking me?
Your thanks will be your belief.
Your thanks is your fatherhood.

Those words made the tears in his eyes overflow, and pour down his cheeks. He repeated to himself, "Your thanks is your fatherhood..."
Wow.
He didn't want this to end, there were so many questions left to ask, but his mind couldn't think of any. He sat, mesmerized by what was happening and by the things Ellis was saying to him. He composed himself and instead of asking more questions, just waited for more magical words to appear in front of him.

To the moon...and back says:
So you are curious what happens after death...
When we pass, we return to the universal energy and love.
That's when we discover that humans are all connected.

Some of us... more than others.
And that begins to answer your question... "Why me?"

CALVIN says:
Wow...

It sounded so ethereal yet made perfect sense. He typed more.

CALVIN says:
 How can I see you again Ellis?

To the moon...and back says:
Feel me.
I can make you feel before I can make you see.
Last night in your office, you felt me all around.
I played with you,
Moving the cold.

CALVIN says:
That was you...

To the moon...and back says:
Give her energy Calvin, I'm draining her.

Ellis kept answering the questions he couldn't even think to ask. But suddenly the realization of whom he was talking with hit him. Hard. This girl had been brutally murdered, and he had to know...

CALVIN says:
Ellis, are you okay now?

To the moon...and back says:
I am fine now.
Back to where I should be.
The path I chose is to help. I'm not done yet.

CALVIN says:
That makes me feel better...

A few minutes passed, and he sat staring blankly at the screen, wondering if her energy had run out or if Jack had come and woken Elizabeth from whatever state she was in.

Then another blink on the screen, and a message.

To the moon...and back says:
Your kids have my love.
My protection.

CALVIN says:
Will we speak again?

To the moon...and back says:
You will feel me.
But I can't tell you where this will go.
There are things we are bound to keep.
We cannot affect others' free will

There are things we are bound to keep.

He repeated that phrase to himself. So much of what he was reading made sense, yet so much was shrouded in mystery. He wanted all the answers and wanted them immediately. But it seemed Ellis was giving him just enough to satiate him, yet keep him guessing as to what this was all about. He obviously wasn't going to get the answers tonight, so he typed the only thing he could think of next.

CALVIN says:
Ellis, can you let others like you know I can help them? Or try?

To the moon...and back says:
They already know. They've known for ages.
Your home will be protected.
Your family will be guarded.
You however, are open.
It's the risk you take when you awaken.
You're a veritable beacon now Calvin.

Those words made him beam with pride. Then he thought of one more question he wanted to ask, one that might help confirm these wild and strange events.

CALVIN says:
I have to know, how'd you send the fax?

He thought he'd be able to determine if this was a hoax by how quickly an answer came through, since that wouldn't be an easy question for which to make up an answer. To his relative surprise, an answer came almost immediately.

To the moon...and back says:
Channels.
Electricity flows through conduits.
I simply find an outlet,
One heading to the source I need.

That satisfied him, and seemed to make as much sense as anything else he'd heard tonight.

That's when he heard the garage door opening. He quickly saved a copy of the conversation to remember exactly what the powerful words were that he'd read. He didn't know if anything like that would ever happen again and wanted to remember it exactly as it happened.

Lisa entered the house through the laundry room and saw him on the computer as he closed out of Messenger.

"What were you doing?" she asked accusingly.

He was still in a state of amazement and lost in thought. All he could say was, "Ellis."

"What?"

"Ellis," he repeated, "I just had a conversation with Ellis."

With that, he opened up the file he just saved for Lisa to read. Then he went to check on the kids, who had been oddly quiet the entire time he was online.

On his way down the hall, reality kicked in and he wondered what Lisa's reaction would be. Would she be mad at him? He also knew he had been on the computer for much longer than intended, and had not made any attempt at starting anything for dinner. He'd certainly hear about that.

Then he remembered he'd forgotten to try and snap Elizabeth out of her trance. He hoped Jack would notice and take good care of her.

...

At bedtime Calvin wanted to read one certain book to the kids. He pulled "Guess How Much I Love You" out of the bookcase in Sterling's room, and with both children gathered on his son's bed, he read the book slowly and thoroughly, as opposed to the break-neck speed that story time had turned into lately; just a part of the race to get the kids to bed on time. The last line of the book resonated in his head as he shut the book: "I love you right up to the moon... and back."

With the kids in bed, Lisa finally had her opportunity to ask the many questions that had obviously been waiting to explode past her lips.

"So, how did you two even start talking? Did she somehow let you know that you needed to get on the computer?"

He didn't know quite how to answer that one without getting himself into trouble. He didn't want to be deceitful; he just didn't think that Lisa would like it if he told her he had hurried home to see if Elizabeth was online. He kept it vague and used the out she had given him in her question.

"Well, yeah. She just happened to be there on the computer when I turned it on. I wanted to check email."

Lisa appeared satisfied with that answer much to his relief, evidently not making the connection that she wouldn't have seen him online if he hadn't set up a chat so she could do so.

"That was wild about her name 'to the moon... and back.' How could Elizabeth or Ellis possibly know that?" she queried.

"Well, I think Ellis is here more often than we realize it. I did know what she was talking about, that day on the stairs when she told me to stop. I thought that it was just my imagination at the time....but wow... it was Ellis!"

It still was such an amazing thing to him.

"Incredible..." he said.

"What did she mean by rearrange the children's rooms? Sleep will be more sound? It sounds almost like Feng Shui," Lisa leaned back and looked perplexed.

"Maybe," Lisa continued, "She is talking about Sterling's nightmares. Do you think? I'll do anything to help Sterling. He's got to be getting exhausted after so many nights of unsettled sleep..."

That would do it for Lisa's questioning for the night. Once she got something in her mind to do, it was like a mission that could not be ignored until she had her questions answered. He was relieved that they weren't going to discuss this all night. He really just wanted to think to himself.

Soon Lisa was off in the bedroom making a call to her sister to ask about Feng Shui design.

Calvin relaxed on the couch, and quickly fell asleep. Lisa woke him later wanting to chat about her conversation.

"I'm off the phone now," she said.

"What? Oh, What did you find out?" he asked.

"Well get this, turns out that Sterling's bed is oriented the way the ancients laid out their dead; feet to the door for easy flow of the spirit on its way out. It creeps me out actually. And we're not supposed to have toys under the bed either because it disturbs some flow from Earth or something like that. We'll have to do some thinking, and try to rearrange stuff tomorrow. But, it's late now, let's just go to bed," said Lisa.

Fatigue finally started to slow Lisa down. Calvin knew if there were anyway she could get into Sterling's room now, she probably would get her second wind and tackle the rearranging. But, it would have to be that way for one more night and then she would make sure that things were moved around before he had a chance for yet another nightmare. Sure enough, just as they settled into bed, Sterling began to sob.

"Daddy!" he wailed.

Thoroughly feeling the depths of his exhaustion, Calvin quickly but heavily made his way to his son's bedroom. He hoped that some daddy hugs and kisses would be enough to soothe his fears and help him back to sleep again. He also hoped that Hannah would remain undisturbed by this loud and heart-wrenching late-night crying.

Chapter 10
Worlds Collide
Friday, December 16, 2005

With Calvin still in the kitchen finishing up the dishes, Lisa answered the knock at the door to find Elizabeth and Jack standing on the doorstep against the backdrop of the cold snowy night. Elizabeth held two small gift bags and Jack clasped a bottle of wine in his gloved hands.

Elizabeth wore an electric blue button down shirt and black leggings tucked into tall boots. Her blonde hair was twisted back into two buns, and the blue of her eyes reflected in the incandescent porch lighting. Jack's wide grin showed his perfectly white teeth. He had an olive complexion, brown hair, and big deep brown eyes. Lisa's five-foot-eight frame was taller than Jack's, who stood slightly pudgy at about five-six.

"Hi, come in," Lisa said as she held the glass storm door open for them. "I'm Lisa, nice to finally meet you guys!"

Elizabeth crossed into the entryway, followed by Jack, and gave Lisa a hug.

"It's so nice to meet you too!"

Lisa didn't come from a family of huggers. For her, a cold and stiff handshake would have sufficed.

Noticing Jack standing in the doorway as Elizabeth and Lisa talked, Calvin closed the dishwasher door and made his way over to introduce himself.

"I'm Calvin," he said, shaking Jack's hand and taking the wine bottle that Jack offered. "Let's get out of the entryway and sit down."

Upon hearing guests arrive, Sterling and Hannah ran to the door. Sterling froze when he saw people he didn't know, but when Elizabeth held one of the gift bags out for him, he gladly approached her and took it.

"Sterling, these are our new friends Elizabeth and Jack," Lisa said. "Why don't you say thank you for the present?"

Sterling muttered a quick 'thanks' shyly under his breath and ran to the couch in the living room to open the gift. Hannah soon joined him with her bag. Sterling's contained a toy car and foaming Spider Man bubble bath, while Hannah's had a soft stuffed Hello Kitty. They also gave the kids two little teddy bears with magnetic noses and scarves wrapped around their necks. The kids were both thrilled with the presents, and played with their new toys as the adults sat down. Elizabeth and Jack settled on the couch, while Lisa and Calvin sat down on the floor in front of the Christmas tree.

Lisa cleared her throat slightly before speaking. "Well that wasn't necessary guys," she said, "But it sure got them over the shyness, didn't it?"

Lisa giggled as Sterling played with his new car on Jack's lap.

The conversation flowed as easily as the wine, as the couples discussed everything from their jobs to their past vacations to their future plans. After an hour, Lisa excused herself to put the kids to bed.

...

"You have a beautiful aura Lisa," Elizabeth said, as she returned from putting the children down.

"I do? Well... thank you. I have heard about auras, but I don't really know anything about them. What does it look like? What does it mean?"

Elizabeth took a sideways glance at Jack and giggled slightly, clasping her hands excitedly together.

She grinned, and said, "I love this stuff. Auras are basically a person's energy field. The colors of the auras around the head have very special meanings. I can tell a lot about you just by looking at your aura. By watching someone's aura, a person can actually see his or her thought process. It helps to determine if the person is telling the truth, or if the words coming out don't match the energy. When you can see an aura, you can see a lie. An aura can't be faked. It shows a person's true nature, and his or her true intent."

Lisa shifted uncomfortably. She knew that she would have to be honest with Elizabeth from the beginning. Almost as if Jack heard her thoughts, he chimed in. "I've stopped trying to get anything past Elizabeth. It's not even worth it. She knows if I lie to her."

"It's true!" she said, "Our auras are our spiritual signature too. So, let's see. Your aura is very bright and the colors shimmer, it's quite beautiful, really very beautiful."

Elizabeth's blue eyes shimmered below eyelashes darkened by mascara. She looked at the space around Lisa's head.

"What about my kids? What do you see with them?" she asked.

"Really?" she was really getting excited now.

"Okay, first your little girl. Hannah's aura is also amazing. It is bright and shimmery. She has lots of pastels, pinks and purples. She is a whimsical little being who will love magic and music and be a free-spirit. She also is inclined toward the healing path, but may follow that in a non-traditional sense. She is your little hippie. She will love music and dancing. She is confident and pure, delicate and elegant. She will probably have trouble with girls as friends because of this. She will be so confident that other girls will be catty toward her. 'Cause girls are just mean. So instead, she'll probably have a small group of close friends. More boys than girls."

"Oh great." Calvin exclaimed, "I was already dreading having a teenage daughter!"

They all laughed. Again, Elizabeth appeared to be hitting it right on with their little Hannah. It was exactly the impression of her personality he thought. Elizabeth continued, "Your son. He is more factual, and analytical. He will probably have a large group of guy friends. And Hannah will probably end up wanting to date some of them. He will be protective of her. He is smart, and will be very successful in school. He's your little businessman. I could see him running a large business; you know, like being the CEO of a Fortune 500 or something! Friends will want to gather around him, and you will probably find that your house is the place where they all want to hang out."

That pleased Calvin. He would rather have ten kids over in the basement with his son, than have him constantly over at someone else's house. This was something important to him, something he had already discussed with Lisa. Again, Elizabeth seemed to hit the nail right on the head in describing the differences that were already pretty apparent between Hannah and Sterling's personalities.

"And Cal," Elizabeth continued as she looked toward him with a sly grin, "You have a fantastic golden border around your aura. It is really incredible. Gold reflects dynamic spiritual energy and a true coming-into-one's-own power. But you would probably already know that. You can see them can't you?"

"No," he replied.

"You can't?" Elizabeth seemed astounded. She sat and thought for a moment. "Do you have trouble with colors?"

Calvin sheepishly replied, "I'm actually colorblind...at least with some reds and greens."

"Well, that's why you can't see them then. If you weren't, then you would be able to, I'm sure of it," said Elizabeth.

She continued, turning to Lisa and saying, "I have to tell you, I feel like I've found a lost brother in Calvin. Almost like we were separated at birth!"

Lisa smiled uncomfortably then replied, "I have no idea what this connection is or why it's happening. I just know Calvin has always had weird things happen to him. Nothing odd has happened in the last few years, until he met you. That seemed to set off this crazy series of events, which has led as all here. It's just almost... unbelievable, you know?"

Her voice trailed off as though processing what to say next.

"I know Lisa," Elizabeth said, "And I have some theories I can talk about tonight."

Cal chimed in, "Like Lisa said, this all very new. Since we met, actually intermittently through my whole life, I've been feeling... presences. Or I'll see things with my eyes closed, and sometimes even hear whispers. But that doesn't help at all because I can't ever make them out."

Elizabeth replied, "Most psychics... dear God I hate that word, but it fits us.... anyway, most are inclined to shine in one area. However I'm guessing that you will be able to shine in most areas. You are clairvoyant, clairaudient, an empath, and eventually, I think, a channeler. You'll learn to decipher those whispers. You'll learn what the slightest image or gesture means. When this first started for me, I was just like okay...great...I see a rose. But over time I'd learn...hey, a rose relates to love. Then I learned to look closer...is it a red rose? A white rose? Is it a bloom or a full flower? Each has its own meaning."

"So let's say this..." Calvin was getting more excited to talk about this with someone who obviously had some experience.

"Say you're with Jack's family, and they know nothing about your abilities. But something happens... a message comes through, or you feel something... and you have to say it. What do you do?"

"Well, that's actually happened."

Jack seemed to know what story his wife was about to tell.

"Before our wedding, Jack's great aunt Sally was diagnosed with lung cancer. She lived with his grandparents at the time. She was so frail the day of our wedding that she couldn't come. His grandparents came of course, but I had to tell Jack about an hour before the ceremony that they NEEDED to take about an hour during the reception to go check on Sally. I didn't want to say anything for fear that they would think I was nuts, or that they just wouldn't believe me. But it was important. So I took a risk. I said, 'Grandma, Sally is going to need you to go check on her for about an hour. Please go to her and know that Jack and I are okay with you not being here for that time. We love you, it's important.' She actually listened. And when she got there, Sally knew she was passing. She was able to give her last wishes. She held on that night, but when they got home from the reception she wasn't able to speak. Bless her heart, she waited until the day after our wedding to pass away so our day wouldn't be interrupted or ruined. It was the best wedding gift we had received." The room fell silent for a few seconds, as everyone absorbed the story. Calvin took advantage of the break in conversation to pour more wine for their guests. He thought about the story, wondering how she could have known.

But at this point the 'how' wasn't nearly as relevant as the 'why,' and that part was obvious.

Lisa took advantage of the silence to begin another story, and ask Elizabeth her thoughts.

"Maybe you can help me understand this Elizabeth..." she said, "A few weeks ago I was changing Hannah's diaper. She was having a fit, I mean kicking her legs and screaming. I had her on her back, struggling to keep her in one place, when she went silent. I could see her eyes latch onto something and follow it. She said, 'Hi....' and giggled. I was able to get her pants back on, then she stood up and ran down the hall, turned to the staircase and pointed down the stairs, like she wanted me to take her down there to follow something..."

Elizabeth giggled in delight. "Yes, I saw something almost as soon as I entered your house tonight. There is a very bright, very playful spirit in your home. Tall, female, not human. She's more of an energy entity than something that ever lived. It's what Hannah laughs at. 'She' is what Hannah follows."

"Sweet!" I said, "What is it? Does it want anything? What's it attached to? It must be attached to something, especially since this is a brand new home! There couldn't be any old ghosts in here."

"First lesson mister..." Elizabeth replied, "Brand new home means crap. You need to take into account the land, the materials that built the home, and most importantly, the items, and the people, IN the home... Granted, you might not get the epic ghosts of yore here... However, you just well might. You need to understand that they are drawn to YOU. Not inherently just here. You know?"

"That makes sense," he said, looking at Lisa as she nodded in agreement.

Elizabeth continued, "The being that Hannah sees is a being of love and light. I'm guessing the experience she chose was to be a child's playmate. She's most likely one of Hannah's spirit guides."

Those words grabbed Calvin's immediate attention. He looked at Elizabeth and said, "Seriously, spirit guides? You're telling me those are real?"

"Really Cal, after everything you've seen with Ellis, does that really surprise you? I think you're quite familiar with the cold sensation when they're around," Elizabeth replied.

He nodded, thinking that Elizabeth seemed to have a real skill at making things that shouldn't make sense sound perfectly reasonable and hard to argue.

"Let me explain the cold feeling really quick," she said, "The cold comes from spirits absorbing and using your energy to manifest. And what is heat, but a type of energy. They can't just exist; they need that energy. Remove or deplete the energy, and what are you left with?"

"Cold," Elizabeth and Calvin said at the same time. Again, there was a pause in the conversation. Elizabeth seemed to be thinking about what to say next. Lisa and Calvin were still taking in what Elizabeth had just said.

Jack took the opportunity to say, "Lisa, if you ever need someone to talk to about this, I'm here. I've been through what you're going through now, and might be able to help you understand."

"Thanks," Lisa replied, "I'll probably take you up on that."

"Calvin, there's something I've wanted to tell you for a while now," Elizabeth said, apparently deciding that now was the time to discuss whatever it was she was thinking about a few seconds earlier.

With everyone's curiosity piqued, she continued, "Vlad the Impaler. Know who that is?"

"Not specifically," he replied, "I've heard the name though."

"Well, his life definitely impacted pop culture and monster lore far and wide! Ever heard of Castle Dracula?" she asked.

"Of course."

"So then you might know that Castle Dracula was one of Vlad the Impaler's fortresses. Vlad is Dracula, or at least the person who inspired Stoker's character," Elizabeth said.

Once again, Elizabeth had him enthralled and he wondered where the hell this conversation was going and how it would relate to the night's conversation.

Elizabeth seemed to sense his hesitation, and said, "Descendants and blood lines, Calvin. Guides. Since the topic has already come up tonight, we might as well talk about what I know."

"What?" he said, "You're telling me that Vlad the Impaler is a guide? Dracula is a guide? Come on..."

"No, he's not a guide," said Elizabeth, "However, one of yours, one of mine... a descendant of Vlad's... is."

"So you're saying not only that spirit guides exist, but you and I actually share one? Who is it? What's his name?" he asked, intrigued by this but wanting to be cautious in believing what Elizabeth was saying. He had to admit though, it sure did explain a lot so far.

"First of all, she would kick you for calling her a he," Elizabeth said, grinning.

"Her name is Seneda. And yes, she is one of my guides as well. She talks through me to Jack."

Calvin looked at Jack, who nodded in validation. "So she channels through you, like Ellis did..." he said, remembering how real that conversation was. "Well how many people meet who share the same guide? How many people do guides look over?"

"Typically, one," Elizabeth replied. "And I've yet to meet another set. I'm still trying to learn why we share one, and what it all means."

"How do you know she's my guide too?"

"I know through dreams," she said. Then she looked at her husband and said, "And a message."

Again, Jack nodded.

"Don't get me wrong," Elizabeth said, "I'm not saying we are vampires or anything...not at all. I'm just saying their roots and origins flow through us. Ancient, dark roots."

He paused, trying to put it all together. Then he spoke again, "So it all goes back to 'Why me?' Is it related to Seneda?"

"Good question," Elizabeth said, "In talking to Jack, who would tell me what he and Seneda talked about, she would tell Jack to remind me that I shouldn't give up, that I should keep searching... for him. That there was another like me out there, somewhere. I've been looking for ages, and I think I've been having dreams about you since I was about three, and more recently I've been getting clues through Jack. That night at the shoot when we met, and you asked about Ellis, I knew I'd found you. I could have died! I've been so excited to find out that you actually exist," she said, appearing to hold back tears.

Lisa's gaze shifted to Jack, who gave her a knowing nod in response.

"It validates a lot for me," Elizabeth said, with a slight quiver in her voice.

"Look Cal," she continued after briefly composing herself, "I believe we share a common bond of a guide to keep us connected, even in times when we couldn't be."

"I think this actually might be starting to make some sense," Calvin said excitedly. "That's why Ellis found me, isn't it? You were best friends, and now she knows you and I share a guide, and we're supposed to do something together. She brought us together."

"That's my theory, too. Networking, so to speak. A chain of events leading us to meet. I'm still trying to wrap my brain around all the maybes," said Elizabeth.

"That fax we got from her, it makes more sense now," he said, getting up and hurriedly moving toward the computer desk in the kitchen. He found the fax in one of the file drawers, and read pieces from it.

"It says, 'You have a lot of work to do, he can help you find out... use your spirit connections... find him...'

"So now the questions are," Calvin said, "What are we supposed to find out, who are we supposed to find and how do we do it?"

Chapter 11
Evil returns
Tuesday, December 20, 2005

Calvin took off his black North Face jacket and threw it onto the beanbag chair in his office. He'd arrived to work early and no one was in the office yet, which was good for having some time alone to get settled.
 He switched on his computer and went to make a pot of coffee while it booted up. Just as he opened the pre-measured bag of coffee grounds, he heard the familiar chime of an instant message coming in from his office.
Jeez, Elizabeth must be up and watching for me this morning.
He hurried into his office to see what she had to say, forgetting to go back and finish making the coffee after he began reading.

To the moon...and back says:
Good morning! Thanks again for Friday night, it was nice seeing you and I know Jack enjoyed meeting Lisa.

He began to wonder how much work time he'd wasted on Instant Messaging over the past few weeks with Elizabeth. But as usual, he typed back.

CALVIN says:
It was fun, wasn't it? I'm glad we finally got everyone together, I think it really helped Lisa understand what's going on. Well, maybe not understand it, but better accept it, I guess. I'm still trying to understand it myself.

To the moon...and back says:
Can you come over today? There's a line of spirits wanting to talk to you...

Calvin didn't know what to say. Part of him wanted to go to her and see what this was all about. The more practical part knew he had a lot of work to get done. Plus, his employees were beginning to arrive and they'd surely ask questions if he left this early in the morning. He assumed they were getting suspicious anyway, with how much time he'd been spending with his office door closed lately. No, he just couldn't get away from work right now.

CALVIN says:
I really can't today. I wish I could.

To the moon...and back says:
Then tonight. I'm at Grace's house until five thirty and have exercise class until 8, can we get together after? There's actually someplace we should go tonight anyway.

He wondered if he should have just accepted the offer to go during work. That would be far easier than telling Lisa he needed to go out with Elizabeth tonight. In fact, she would have never even had to know if he went to see Elizabeth this morning. But regardless, he decided that meeting tonight would be better for his career.

CALVIN says:
That will work. Where?

To the moon...and back says:
Great! I'll pick you up at your house at 8:30. We're going to a cemetery.

"Of course we are," he mumbled aloud."That'll be easy to explain..."

To the moon...and back says:
It's cold in here.

Calvin didn't reply right away, but he didn't need to.

To the moon...and back says:
....

The message was blank aside from a line of dots. He hadn't seen a message like that before. He wrote back to her.

CALVIN says:
Is that you Elizabeth?

To the moon...and back says:
a bright boy

Evidently it wasn't her. His pulse quickened. Who was it this time, and why?

CALVIN says:
Who is this?

To the moon...and back says:
We've yet to speak formally,

Though my wings brushed you as a child.
During your life we have crossed paths. Checking in and out, making sure our charges were still whole.

Calvin began to notice that 'they,' the spirits, were rarely direct in their communication. He wanted a direct answer, but he was also still mesmerized that this was even happening to him.

CALVIN says:
And you are....

To the moon...and back says:
Jade
So my name has been dubbed. Though I do not formally have a name.
Hello little man.

Little man? Is that some kind of insult?
Again, he wanted to get right to the point.

CALVIN says:
What can I do for you?

To the moon...and back says:
What can I do for you?

Obviously being direct wasn't going to get him anywhere. The spirit world apparently didn't have to worry about wasting time or meeting deadlines. He decided he might as well try to learn more about what's been going on, and how to communicate with spirits on his own.

CALVIN says:
What can I do to better see/hear the ones like you?
The ones who try to contact me?

To the moon...and back says:
There is a saying: Ask, seek, and knock.
There's a space you need to find.
Elizabeth calls it static.

CALVIN says:
Yes...

Elizabeth talked about finding her 'static,' and being able to receive messages when in that state. She described it as being half awake, half asleep... just kind of daydreaming but without the thinking. For most of their marriage, Lisa gave Calvin a hard time for "spacing off," to which he'd reply he was just taking some time to "go to the Bahamas," a term he borrowed from comedian Steve Martin.

To the moon...and back says:
Are you actively seeking this static?

CALVIN says:
Yes, I just don't know how to get there.

To the moon...and back says:
There is your problem.

CALVIN says:
Can you help?

To the moon...and back says:

I can try my very best. And that is all I can promise.
My help is at your disposal.
Today, find a relaxing pose;
comfort is key to letting go.
Find that blank stare.
You call it something amusing

Of course, he knew the term of which she spoke...

CALVIN says:
The Bahamas...

To the moon...and back says:
Yes. Find your Bahamas.
With your eyes open, relax your blinking... until it
slows to barely nothing.... you will find
that blurred and blessed vision.
And I will stand in front of you.
Keep your heart and mind open.
You should see me.
You have many others trying to get to you.
Meditation is something you'll need to learn.

CALVIN says:
I understand. I won't see you, or any others, like
Elizabeth does.

To the moon...and back says:
Eventually you will, and stronger than she, Little
Man.

He beamed. Maybe all those years of feeling special, feeling different from others, was valid after all... But still his practical mind, and nearly 30 years of spiritual denial, held him back from fully believing this. The thought was still in his mind that maybe Elizabeth was just crazy, maybe she had multiple personality disorder and he was just getting caught up in her web of madness.

CALVIN says:
Honestly, I need proof. Something that doesn't come through Elizabeth. I want to believe this all...

To the moon...and back says:
Your energy has always been amazing.
Do you recall making the microwave pop?

He instantly flashed back to a day, about six months ago, when he started the microwave and it nearly exploded with a bright flash and loud pop. It seemed so long ago already. Could he have somehow caused that? How could Elizabeth have possibly known that?

To the moon...and back says:
It made me laugh the sweetest laugh, a human laugh.

Still, he had his doubts.

CALVIN says:
You know how skeptical I am... how I quickly dismiss things. The more proof, the better...

To the moon...and back says:
The proof is there for you.

Get your sight aligned.

He was getting sick of meaningless phrases like this.
If the proof was there for him, he obviously wouldn't
need to ask for it.

CALVIN says:
You are all frustrating! I guess I just need to try
harder...

To the moon...and back says:
Or try less
We may seem frustrating to you Little Man, but you
have a life to distract you. We have... you.

He was seeing now that 'Little Man' wasn't meant as
an insult at all, it was just her way of referring to him.
Plus, what she said made sense. Deciding this was his
chance to take advantage and try to get whatever
answers he could, he asked another question.

CALVIN says:
　　　What's it like on your side?

To the moon...and back says:
On my side it is thought.
I know not how to express feeling.
I can tell you the concept of love.
I can tell you the process of compassion.

Again, that seemed to make some sense. He paused,
not knowing what to say next. Jade's next words took
care of that for him.

To the moon...and back says:
I feel you have already seen me?
A bright shimmer,
like tinsel,
like foil.
like the reflection of water.

The blue reflection by the TV. If this was all a hoax, this Elizabeth girl must be a psychic AND have multiple personality disorder. And with all the coincidences so far, he was starting to convince himself this was the real thing. Still, skepticism remained.

CALVIN says:
Yes, I've seen you. Are you a guide to me?

To the moon...and back says:
I am a guide to Jack, a guardian to Elizabeth, and to you.

CALVIN says:
You see my skepticism don't you?

To the moon...and back says:
Yes.
It is welcome.
It shows you are not weak in spirit and also strong in mind.

He accepted that. Then he thought of a question...

CALVIN says:
Do I have other guides? Can you tell me their names?

To the moon...and back says:
You do.
I can.
One you have knowledge of now, yes?

CALVIN says:
Yes. Seneda.

To the moon...and back says:
She has experienced life many times over and finally came back to guide.
Another guide is Seamus.
Who was alive as well.
A shepard's son turned warrior.
Pagan and strong.
It's through him your resistance to Christianity flows.

He chuckled to himself, as the word 'resistance' seemed like an understatement. But he was proud, albeit a little intimidated, at hearing the words 'warrior' and 'pagan.' Like many others, he associated paganism with witchcraft and looked forward to learning the truth about it.
For now though, he was content with the knowledge of having his guides' names. He figured he'd be hearing from them sooner or later.
He stared into the screen, anxiously waiting for more from Jade. Another message blinked onto the screen.

To the moon...and back says:
You've always yearned to please a crowd. You started with those two.

In your parents' bed, as a child, you saw them first and you felt their reaction to your smile.
Ask your mother.
She will tell you about your random laughter as an infant and young child
And how she knew you were entertaining guests.

He made a mental note to ask his mom about that.
He also started thinking that he really needed to get to work.

To the moon...and back says:
You are rushed.

CALVIN says:
Yes. Is there anything else I need to know?

To the moon...and back says:
That is up to you.
Knowledge is yours for the taking.
Knowledge is something we all have, as we all come from it.
It's just a matter of remembering.

CALVIN says:
Just remember... I need validation on this... signs that are undeniable to me. And, I'm sorry to say... signs that are obvious....

To the moon...and back says:
You always have had to be hit in the head.
We expected nothing less this time.

He let out an audible chuckle, and knew she had a point.

To the moon...and back says:
Just remember, we don't always have the answers.
We work with our charges to complete the puzzle.
So let's work together.
We will try our best to give you obvious signs,
And you try to not give up.
We need you, more than you know right now.

CALVIN says:
I promise to not give up.

To the moon...and back says:
And your suspicions of the man in the office... the new one... why do you doubt?
Use your intuition here Little Man.
Your knowledge.
He isn't to be trusted by the way, the new one.
The new employee.
But you know that

CALVIN says:
Whoa.

Calvin's boss had recently made a new hire in his department, without his input. The guy's name was John and Calvin had been suspicious of him since day one.

To the moon...and back says:
You ask for proof... we give it.

Realization that you were right should be sparking your energy in your hands.

He looked at his hands, expecting to see something obvious this time. He didn't.

CALVIN says:
I might be a moron, but all I see are fingertips. See my frustration?

To the moon...and back says:
But you did see.
In your mind you saw the blue lines and tracers.
But you said 'No, that's in my mind.'
And this is your problem.
Seeing is beyond the realm of pure vision.
When you look straight at a star it will stop twinkling, correct?
Look at it sideways, or through reflection and it twinkles with no end.
It's the perception and acceptance of the view of energy.
WE are energy.
How can you see us if you look straight on?
We will stop twinkling.

With this, more of his skepticism faded. The eloquence and beauty with which spirits spoke was enlightening and inspiring. He figured this is why Jade came through this morning, this is what he needed to hear.

CALVIN says:
The movements from the corner of my eyes...

To the moon...and back says:
Yes.
You ask all the time and
we twinkle as bright as possible.
And yet you deny us.
Elizabeth doesn't see more than you.
She's just learned to interpret her twinkle.

He sat in front of his computer, dumbfounded, but nodding to himself.

To the moon...and back says:
I leave you with this.
January will be very demanding.
You will have his name soon enough,
It is meant to be.
But like everything, in the right time.
There are things to learn before then.
Doubts to overcome.
Go with Elizabeth tonight. When you see her, she will be wearing an artifact from the past.
I go in peace and love.

He looked at the clock. It was 10:30.

To the moon...and back says:
Hey Cal! Are you there? I somehow just lost 2 hours, I've got to go!

He could feel the shift in energy from Jade's words to Elizabeth's.

CALVIN says:

Yeah, I did too actually. We'll talk about it all tonight! I've got a lot to tell you. Later...

He was shocked to see that two hours had passed since he received the first message this morning from Elizabeth. He was also surprised that no one came to say good morning or had even called, for that matter. He shuddered to think what his employees must be thinking and saying about him. But at the same time, his head spun with more questions. What will be so demanding about January? Whose name would he get?

It occurred to him that whomever Jade referred to today is the same person Ellis meant in the fax, when she said, "Find him." The clues were coming together, and he was excited to talk to Elizabeth about it all, later that night.

...

Calvin waited until dinner to let Lisa know about his plans with Elizabeth. He was initially nervous about what her reaction would be, but the more he thought about it the more he didn't care.

"So Elizabeth has something she needs to show me tonight, and we have some things to talk about. She's picking me up at 8:30," he said.

"Umm...alright..." Lisa replied, "And you think it's okay to just announce your plans without asking if it works for me? Where are you going? When will you be back?"

"Does it really matter? You're just going to put the kids down and go to bed anyway. I'll be home after you fall asleep," he snapped back at her.

Lisa was visibly angered.

"Fine, go do whatever it is you have to do with her."

Lisa paused.

"But Calvin, for my own sanity while you're gone, I want to know where you are going."

"A cemetery," he quickly responded, "How's that for your sanity? Why can't you just say 'Okay Honey, I'll see you when you get back.' Why do you even need the details?"

"A cemetery!? Why the hell do you need to go to a cemetery on a Tuesday night? And yeah, I want the details because that's what spouses are supposed to get!" Lisa's anger exploded.

"I don't know exactly," Calvin answered quietly, feeling some guilt for the way he just spoke to her. Then he remembered something Jade had said earlier.

"But I do know the spirits need me for something important, and tonight should shed some light on that."

"Whatever Calvin," Lisa said dismissively.

"Lisa, I talked to a new one today. Actually, one I saw by the TV a while ago at night. Her name is Jade." He hoped this would calm her down a little.

"Whatever. Have fun on your little date," she said.

They hardly spoke to each other through the rest of dinner. Calvin got himself ready to go as Lisa put the kids to bed. Soon it was 9 o'clock, with no word from Elizabeth.

"Looks like you're little girlfriend is late," Lisa said sarcastically.

"Girlfriend? Where did that come from? She'll be here," he said shortly.

"I'm going to bed. See you when I see you I guess." Lisa turned to walk down the hallway toward their bedroom.

Calvin sat on the couch and turned on the TV. Fighting with Lisa didn't feel good and now he was concerned that Elizabeth was so late. She still hadn't shown up by 10:30. Lisa apparently heard the TV still on and came back out into the living room.

"Holy shit, she's not here yet? You're not still going are you? You have to work tomorrow. You could've been back by now if she was actually on time! Nice to see she's so responsible and courteous," Lisa said, again in her most sarcastic tone.

Calvin's phone rang, and Elizabeth's number showed up on the caller ID. He answered.

"Hey Elizabeth- you still coming?"

"Yes! I'm so sorry," she replied, "My friend Melinda had a small car accident so I went to help her, then I realized I'd left my phone at the gym when I went to call you. Can you still come?"

"Yeah, I can still come," he said, looking directly at Lisa. She glared back at him then turned back toward their bedroom.

Thirty minutes later he and Elizabeth were on their way to a cemetery on the other side of the city. He told Elizabeth every detail he could remember about the conversation with Jade.

"It still feels really weird to know I was sitting there typing, but have no memory of anything I said. When spirits channel through me, I just leave. I'm gone. They completely take over my body. It's disturbing really, that they can do that so easily," she said.

"I can't imagine Elizabeth..."

"Well, it sure is nice to finally have someone who understands me, and who accepts me without asking too many questions. I'm glad you came into my life Calvin."

He looked at her.

"Actually," he said, "I think it's you who came into MY life."

Elizabeth turned the car into the driveway and through the open gates of the Moran Prairie Cemetery. It was a fairly small cemetery, maybe a hundred yards long by as many wide. The main road divided the cemetery in half, then made a T at the end where another road circled it. They sat silent as Elizabeth drove to the end of the main road and stopped the car.

"Well, this is it," she said, "What do you think?"

"It's beautiful," he replied. A few inches of freshly fallen snow blanketed the grounds, with the old dark headstones providing a jagged contrast to the bright, smooth snow.

"Let's walk around," said Elizabeth.

He opened his door and stepped outside. It was colder than he'd thought it would be, and he wished he'd remembered to bring gloves. He shoved his hands into the pockets of his jacket and waited for Elizabeth to come meet him. Together they walked out onto the cemetery grounds, without a sound except for the snow crunching under their feet.

"What is out here that you wanted to show me?" he asked.

"Just, this," she said, looking around, "Just stop, be aware, breathe, watch, and listen. Things ALWAYS happen at this cemetery."

His heart beat faster in anticipation of seeing something, and in fear of what that something might be. Elizabeth nudged him in the arm.

"Look," she said, pointing off to her left.

He looked in the direction she pointed.

"What? I don't see anything..."

"Look closer... at those footprints," Elizabeth said, "This is part of your problem Calvin, you don't pay attention to the details, and when you skip the details, you miss so much."

He paid special attention to the footprints she gestured toward.

"They're barefoot..." he said.

"Yes, and..." she continued, "They just start and stop at random. No tracks coming or going. Just... roaming footprints. That's why I like this cemetery so much. Especially in the winter."

He shivered, and not from the cold. Evidently Elizabeth had spent a lot of time here, which kind of freaked him out a little.

"Be aware," Elizabeth said, "Always look closely at things, because often, they're not what they seem."

That thought circled in his head as he stared at the random prints in the snow.

"Jesus, Elizabeth... look!" he suddenly exclaimed.

He pointed at new footprints, being formed directly in front of them. He could hardly believe his eyes, but right there was more proof that this entire series of events was not the concoction of a mad woman's mind.

Elizabeth just grinned and nodded as they watched the footprints, starting and stopping at random. They mesmerized him, without a thought in his mind other than watching spirits roam from tombstone to tombstone.

Elizabeth looked up while he continued staring down.

"And," she said blissfully after a few seconds, "Never focus your eyes in one direction for too long, because you'll never know what you're missing..."

He looked ahead, and his jaw dropped. Hovering a few feet off the ground was a blue shimmering being, which almost looked like the reflection of water.

"Jade..." he said.

"Still looking for proof, Little Man?" she said. Instead of hearing her words, it's more like they were said directly inside his head. Elizabeth didn't look nearly as surprised as he felt. He had to assume she'd seen something like this before.

Elizabeth turned to him and said, "She won't have long here, she's feeding off our energy to appear to us. This is why we came to this cemetery, there is very little outside energy to disrupt her. You won't see them like this very often."

He heard Jade's words again, "Did you see the artifact?"

He had completely forgotten to even look for an artifact from his past that Elizabeth might be wearing.

"Not YOUR past... at least not the past you can remember," Jade said. "Her necklace."

Elizabeth pulled the necklace she wore out of her coat, equally as surprised that Jade would mention it.

"My sister found this for me," Elizabeth said, "In an antique shop in Ireland last summer. She said it reminded her of me."

Jade spoke again.

"There's a reason for that. Listen to me carefully. You are two of the oldest, most potent spirits living on Earth right now. And this isn't your first lifetime existing together."

Calvin and Elizabeth looked at each other, both equally amazed, then turned their attention back to the spirit in front of them.

"You lived in Ireland, ages ago, together. Little Man, you gave Elizabeth THAT necklace as a gift. Your friend Seamus actually helped you pick it out…"

They looked back at each other in shock as a reason for their incredible connection became infinitely clearer. In his short time of knowing Elizabeth, he had never seen her react in such surprise.

"So after all those years, it survived, and ended up in an antique shop in Ireland? And my sister just happened to find it? This is incredible…" said Elizabeth.

"Not incredible," said Jade, "Guides can be very compelling."

"I mentioned that January will be demanding," she continued, not giving them ample time to digest this new information, "And I don't say that lightly. You will need that relic. There IS magic in this world; some darker and more powerful than you can ever imagine. On the next full moon, you'll need the relic and a drop of blood from each of you…"

Jade's voice trailed off, as though she wasn't able to finish her thought.

"What? Why? What do we need to do? Jade!" Calvin yelled.

But she was gone.

He felt the shift immediately. Dark came in over him. No, more than dark. He could feel it again. Suffocating evil. It was the same feeling he had 10 years ago in the car with Lisa. His chest tightened and his body wanted to sweat but couldn't. He felt like all moisture had been wrung out of him, leaving him bone dry yet clammy. An ominous, evil presence was close. Even speaking was difficult. "Elizabeth, we've got to go, now! You feel that? This is the feeling, the same evil feeling on the night of Pitchfork Man. He's here. Whoever he is, he's here and we have to go."

Elizabeth didn't respond. She just stood frozen, her shoulders oddly slumped forward, but her eyes staring straight ahead. He quickly saw what she was looking at. They didn't look like ordinary hooded or cloaked humans, but had that same shape. They were absolute recesses of blackness, like holes in the dark night. They reminded him of the classic and hauntingly familiar image of Death. And they approached fast.

He got directly in front of Elizabeth's face and screamed "RUN!"

She snapped out of her trance, and he grabbed her hand. They sprinted to the car, but before Elizabeth could get it started, the car shook violently. The knocks of what sounded like 10,000 fists pounded the car, and he begged Elizabeth to get the car started. She did, and they sped out of the cemetery.

They didn't speak and hardly even breathed until arriving in the busiest most well-lit section of downtown they could find.

Elizabeth pulled over to the side of the road under a street lamp. It immediately popped, and went out. Panting in fear, they looked at each other, hearts still pumping adrenaline through their bodies. Although they both noticed the light go out, they had much bigger things to worry about.

"What... the...HELL... was that?" Calvin asked.

"That," Elizabeth replied, "Was evil. That...must be what we are supposed to stop."

"Jesus," he said, "And I thought finding Ellis's murderer would be bad..."

"We've got a lot to think about Cal. This is bigger than I could have ever thought. Jade mentioned the full moon...When is the next one?"

Elizabeth reached across him to her glove box and pulled out a pocket calendar to answer her own question, "January 14th."

"Don't you dare lose that necklace between now and then," he said while glancing at the dashboard clock. "Christ, it's almost 2:30. I've got to get home. How am I going to explain this?"

"Some things you don't need to explain, Cal. Some things will only freak her out more than help her," she offered. "Some secrets are okay."

The drive home was silent. Calvin tried not to forget the beauty of seeing and talking to Jade, even though for obvious reasons his mind was on other things. More street lamps extinguished above as they drove.

"That always happens to me," Elizabeth said, glancing up at the darkened lights.

"Me too," Calvin said.

She looked at him and said, "What if that is our sign? That they are always with us?"

He nodded as Elizabeth pulled into his driveway and stopped the car. He took a deep breath to speak, but didn't know what to say. He just reached over and hugged her, then left the car without saying a word. Instead of walking into a quiet and sleepy house, he could hear his wife sobbing in the bedroom.

"Goddammit," he thought, immediately overcome with anger rather than compassion. He didn't want to deal with her tonight. He just wanted to fall asleep.

"Two fucking thirty!?" Lisa screamed, "I've been going bat-shit crazy wondering what the hell you are doing in the middle of the God damn night in a CEMETERY until 2:30 in the morning! Why the hell didn't you answer your phone?"

"My phone was on silent, I'm sorry. Tonight was..." he paused while debating on what to tell her, "Beautiful. I saw actual spirits, I saw footprints forming in the snow, it was amazing."

"Well I hope the footprints were worth it to you. I can't do this for long Calvin, I can't put up with this, with you just leaving like that. I can't," she said as her voice broke into sobs.

"You don't have to Lisa," he said as he wrapped his arms around her, "This will all be over on January 14th. I don't know all the details yet, but that's the day I do whatever it is I'm supposed to do."

Lisa looked at him with her big round exhausted eyes.

"Until then, I'm probably going to have to go places without a lot of explanation. I'm going to need your support."

"I'll try," said Lisa.

"Thanks, let's get to bed," he said, relieved that this ended so quickly.

...

Six thirty in the morning came way too fast. They both dragged themselves out of bed, not saying a word about the previous night. They got the kids ready and headed out.

Calvin arrived at work still half asleep. Luckily this time there was coffee made already. He grabbed a cup, said good morning to his staff, and closed himself in his office, expecting a recap through IM with Elizabeth.

Sure enough, the icon next to her name signaled that she was online. His heart skipped a beat from excitement and he sent her a note even before opening up his work email.

CALVIN says:
Good morning, you're sure up early! What a night...

He waited for a response. Nothing. He opened his email while he waited. Then his screen blinked.

To the moon...and back says:
....

CALVIN says:
Who's coming through?

To the moon...and back says:
Samael

Calvin didn't recognize the name, but didn't like it. A new message popped up.

To the moon...and back says:
That's his name.

CALVIN says:
Who is this?

To the moon...and back says:
Brotherhood never needs be asked ye git.

And it was obvious. He was speaking with one of his guides, and, apparently, an old friend from another life. Completely mind-boggling.

CALVIN says:
Seamus?

To the moon...and back says:
Aye, ye arse

He just called me an ass.

Calvin was fascinated that each spirit he'd communicated with so far had his/her own language and own personality, even through the relative anonymity of instant message. He stared at the screen, again not exactly knowing what to say to properly greet a spirit.

To the moon...and back says:
a warning, friend.

Calvin's heart sank. This was going to be serious. And if a pagan warrior was giving warnings, he sure as hell was going to listen. Scared out of his mind, but intent on learning why, he waited and listened.

To the moon...and back says:
Samael brings death.

Calvin's heart skipped a thousand beats at the word 'death.'

To the moon...and back says:
And when death be avoided, his ire be raised.
Don't think it's a mishap or chance that you two pulled out of there last night alive.

Calvin was afraid. The novelty of everything being so new was wearing off. The reality of it all was no longer questioned, but his ability to deal with it was.

To the moon...and back says:
Had she been there alone, he would have taken her. You saved her, now he wants you too, ye git.

CALVIN says:
What should we do?

To the moon...and back says:
Don't ye dare give in.
An don't give up either.

CALVIN says:
Never.

To the moon...and back says:
Samael wants you two torn apart.
It wants you because you're the one person who can save her. And together, you're the only two who can prevent it from achieving its goal.

He noticed that Seamus was referring to this Samael as 'it.' That couldn't be a good sign.

To the moon...and back says:
It would be a shame to have you come back to this side so early. You can save and touch many a life.

He desperately wanted to know what was happening. How could he possibly save lives?
If he'd learned one thing so far, it's that the answers come with time. Right now, he just wanted to lighten the mood somehow...and since Jade told him they had experienced life together in the past, he wanted to know more.

CALVIN says:
    Can I ask you something?

To the moon...and back says:
    Aye, anythin'

CALVIN says:
Where did we live in Ireland?

To the moon...and back says:
    Waterford.
Do ye remember my girl?

Calvin chuckled. *Of course not... how could I?*

To the moon...and back says:
Her name was Ansel.
A fair beaut in her own right.
my girl,
my heart.
Her eyes, dark as the raven.
And when they would tear up because of the arse of a husband and tyrant she was married to, I would light like fire.

Ah... he fell in love with a married woman.

CALVIN says:
But at least you're with her now, right?

To the moon...and back says:
No.
She chose to be done.
The pain of losing true love was her last. She couldn't bear to go through it again. A consequence of my sacrifice.

The ringing of his office phone interrupted him, and he instinctively copied the message and then shut down the messenger. He felt bad for suddenly disappearing and wanted to know more about Seamus.

The break from the spiritual realm didn't last long as the name "Samael" echoed in his head. Could that be the spirit who came to him back in 1995? Up until now, it was the one experience from his past that terrified him, and to have a name he could attach to the experience was surreal, and frightening. Why was it back? What did it want? Why did it care whether or not he had become friends with Elizabeth? Why did it leave him alone for 10 years?

He entered the name in Google and began reading some of the articles on this 'mythical' being.

"Samael is an important figure in lore, a figure who is accuser, seducer, and destroyer. Legends mentioning Satan refer equally to him, such that Samael is often taken to be the true or angelic name of the Devil."

From his experiences so far, Calvin thought that sounded about right.
He read on, terrified.

"The etymology of Samael is "Venom of God," as he is sometimes identified with the Angel of death."

With that he had read enough and wanted to discuss his findings with Elizabeth. He pulled her up on IM again. Not surprisingly, she was still there.

CALVIN says:
Elizabeth? You there? I want to send you something. You have time for some reading?

To the moon...and back says:
No. But you are reading.

It didn't feel like Elizabeth, something was missing from her response. It felt too...cold.

CALVIN says:
Elizabeth?

To the moon...and back says:
It's a nice name.

CALVIN says:
Who's there?

His pulse quickened and his stomach churned as his gut seemed to know the answer already.

To the moon...and back says:
Though I'm more drawn to older names.

CALVIN says:
Who is this?

He wanted to give whomever it was time to identify itself before he tried to call Elizabeth back.

To the moon...and back says:
I really don't like questions.
Challenging, aren't you?

CALVIN says:
I need to know who you are.

To the moon...and back says:
You need to know do you?

And what does your study of choice tell you?

He stood up from his chair and yelled, "No! Get out of her!"

Quickly realizing he was screaming at his monitor, he dialed Elizabeth's cell number, not sure what to expect on the other end. To his relief, Jack answered.

"Jack, it's Calvin. Look, you need to go get Elizabeth back, now," he said.

"What? Is she okay?" he replied.

"Just do it, Jack, trust me."

"Sure, hang on," he said.

A half minute passed before Jack came back.

"Jesus Christ, what was that?" Jack asked, "She's beat. No energy, no color... and her eyes... they lost their blue."

"Is she okay?" he asked.

"Yeah, she's fine. At least she's Elizabeth again. But seriously, her eyes were totally black. I've never seen her like that before. What was that?"

Calvin breathed a sigh of relief knowing Samael was gone again, for now.

"That," he said, "Was something we need to get rid of. It's going to be a rough couple of weeks."

Chapter 12
The Christmas Feeling
Sunday, December 25, 2005

As much as Calvin loved Christmas, it exhausted him. All the excitement of the day finally caught up with the kids too, and they were fast asleep in bed soon after they returned home from Calvin's parents' house.

Lisa had lit a candle on the dresser in the master bedroom and went to take a bubble bath in the jetted Jacuzzi tub. Calvin flopped himself into a fabric armchair in the room's sitting area and closed his eyes.

For the first time that day, he was alone with some silence. He remembered the conversation from earlier in the month about Elizabeth's birthday... he didn't want her to think the 'carpenter's birthday' overshadowed hers. He reached for his phone and dialed her number, keeping the conversation short so Lisa wouldn't catch him on the phone.

It was a short and sweet conversation and after he hung up, he found himself watching the flame of the candle dance, mesmerized by the way it seemed to stay perfectly still, then erupt in a flicker of activity. As his stare intensified, an energy field surrounded the flame like an iridescent shadow. He remembered the conversation with Jade.

"Find that blurred and blessed vision..."

He wanted to have a spiritual experience on his own... without Elizabeth there to guide him through it.

Calvin was conscious enough to not stare directly into the shadow of the flame, but to just be aware of it. As he sat staring, he saw what could be interpreted as a face. Rather than dismiss it as something meaningless, he opened himself up to the possibility that it really was a face. As he did, the image lingered, and he noticed more details.

This was not a happy image. The facial expression was frozen, but appeared tortured, in pain, its mouth open in a silent scream. Then it faded away only to be replaced by another, then another. Each face looked more distressed, more hurt, more tortured than the one before it. They looked more like desperate pleas for help rather than anything threatening, so he wasn't scared. It's when they stopped looking human that he finally said aloud, "Okay, stop. I can't handle so many all at once. Enough faces."

Then he saw letters, slowly rising from the candle itself. He could tell there were three letters, but couldn't make out what they were. Sometimes he'd just see the top halves of the letters while others were too blurry and yet others were too far out of his field of vision to see.

His mind sorted through all possibilities of what each letter could be. Was it trying to spell something? What could be spelled with only three letters?

Then for an instant all three letters were visible and clear, directly in front of him... NAB.

He uttered a barely audible, "Nab?" just as the letters transformed into what appeared to be a shrub, sitting directly behind the flame of the candle. This was the last thing he saw before succumbing to exhaustion.

Chapter 13
Revelation
Thursday, December 29, 2005

The week between Christmas and New Year's Eve was usually pretty slow at Calvin's office. Lisa had come down with a severe flu earlier in the week, which forced Calvin to work from home to take care of the kids since their daycare was closed for the week.
There had been little spiritual activity since Christmas night and Calvin hadn't even heard from Elizabeth since he called her four days ago.
He wasn't surprised to hear his cell phone ring as that thought entered his head.
Sure enough, it was her.
"Hey Elizabeth!" he excitedly answered.
"Hey back, mister!" she happily replied.
"It's good to hear from you! I'm sorry I can't talk long right now... just strung between being daddy and working and taking care of sick Lisa," he said.
"I totally understand!" she said, "Take care of what you need to today. I feel bad for Lisa, it's no fun to be sick."
"I have a second now," he said as he stepped into the kitchen, out of earshot from where Lisa slept in the bedroom.
"I have strong feelings today, Cal. Something is stirring," she said, with a sense of urgency now in her voice. She was still chipper, just more serious than when the conversation began. He figured this was the reason she called.
"What do you think it is?"

"I don't know, discord of some kind. And strong. All of my friends are arguing, Jack isn't happy today, his grandma is in the hospital, something is just amiss today," she said.

"I wonder what it could be? Lisa just woke up horribly sick, she can hardly stand up," he agreed.

"The poor girl. I just feel a lull today you know? Chaos perhaps..." she said as her voice trailed off.

"Maybe we can meet tomorrow afternoon?" he asked. He wasn't sure what meeting would accomplish, but every time they'd seen each other so far, they managed to put another piece of the puzzle together.

"I'd love to, if it works for you," Elizabeth said.

"Good," he replied, "I'll make it work."

"Hey," Calvin continued, "Do you remember the name Seamus? Have I mentioned him to you since Jade mentioned him that night?" he asked.

"No. Seamus is the Irish version of James, I think," said Elizabeth.

"Seamus is one of my guides. Apparently he lived with us in Ireland. Which is, quite honestly, a little unbelievable. But I'm beyond the point of questioning what reality is at this point."

"Amazing how one's perception of reality changes as he gains knowledge, isn't it?" she said with her now-familiar giggle. "I wonder why I've never seen Seamus or heard from him?"

"I don't think he likes to come through. Seems like he'd rather observe, unless there's something big he's drawn to," he replied.

Calvin continued, "Anyway, he said he was in love with a married woman... I think that he knew he could be killed for loving her... but he didn't care. He took a chance. And, what do you know, he was killed for it."

"That's so sad... killed for true love," said Elizabeth. Then after a pause she said, "You know, sometimes I wonder if it's possible to restore people's faith in love. I don't know... but it's something I've always thought I could do. Maybe that has something to do with the situation we're in."

"What, love?" he asked.

"Finding the truth," Elizabeth said, "About true love. Maybe even finding true love."

Something about the way she said that took him off guard, but excited him. He had to admit, he was developing feelings for this girl. Could she be the one he was meant to be with?

At the same time, he tried to make the connection between true love and Samael, an evil spirit that evidently wanted them dead.

Calvin's thoughts quickly moved to Lisa. Sure, he loved her. He'd always been with her. But was it true love? He thought so at first, but in recent years had questioned it.

He didn't speak.

"So...tell me time frame," Elizabeth said.

"Time frame on what?" he asked.

Calvin began to feel the fear build up in him again as he thought of the spirit they were dealing with.

"Time you have to spare to speak right now," said Elizabeth.

He looked into the living room and saw the kids playing nicely together. "Actually, things have calmed down a little. What's on your mind?"

"I want to read you something, let me find it. Please don't let me keep you from anything... Hey, while I'm searching, what are you and Lisa doing for New Year's Eve?"

"I think we're going to a friend's house for games and fireworks. They have kids too, so we'll let them play. We might even make it until midnight! What are you doing?"

"That sounds like fun," she said, "We're throwing a party. I'll call you at midnight, okay?"

She didn't give him time to respond before adding, "The entity, do you assume it's male or female?"

"Male," he replied.

"Have you seen it again?" she asked, "It kept me from sleeping last night, until about 4 a.m. Then I dreamt of Ireland."

"Well, Ireland makes sense now, knowing what we know. That's a good thing. The entity is not a good thing."

"I just won't give it the info it wants," he said, in a matter of fact manner, "Which sounds insane considering I don't know what it wants yet."

"Just keep talking," she said, "I'm searching now through my book of demons... tons of names to go through," Elizabeth said.

"You have a book of demons?"

"I do, yes indeed," replied Elizabeth. He could hear her flipping through pages, obviously not yet finding what she was looking for. "Did you know that according to Christian theologies, all pagan deities are demons? They think paganism may as well be Satanism. Like they're all baby eaters... isn't that funny?"

"Baby, the other, other white meat," Calvin said, laughing.

Elizabeth, between giggles, continued, "Okay, so some pagans weren't nice... but it's the balance you know?"

"Well, I don't think Catholics are in any position to judge other religions," he said, feeling comfortable enough to say anything he felt to Elizabeth.

"Would our demon even be in a book?" he asked. "Have I even told you what its name is?"

"YOU KNOW ITS NAME!?" Elizabeth yelled urgently before calming herself. "And yes, this particular one is in the book somewhere. You don't tend to draw small things, my dear. But you sure could have saved me some time looking if you would have just told me the name!"

"Samael," he said.

Silence.

Followed by more silence.

"Elizabeth?"

"Oh my God. Oh my God. How could I have been so careless..." she said, then paused for a more few seconds before continuing.

"Hold on, I'm trying to breathe..."

Calvin took this to mean that she did indeed know about Samael, even without her book of demons, and probably knew a lot more than he learned on his quick online search.

Then something occurred to him that both frightened the hell out of him and pissed him off.

"Holy crap Elizabeth... my son's been having terrible dreams, about a man with sharp teeth who comes to get him. The same dream over and over. Could this be connected?"

"Yeah, Cal, it could," she said, still recovering from the shock of hearing the name.

"I actually had a similar experience as a child, I'll tell you about it someday. I feel for your little guy. They may not be just dreams. Keep an eye on him, and watch for any new marks on his skin. Next time I come over I'll look around his room," she said.

Calvin thought he'd keep this information from Lisa for now, as it would only scare her. It sure scared him.

Elizabeth continued, "Okay, when it's around do you feel compelled to... give up? To give in?"

"Hence June 1995. Pitchfork Man, Elizabeth. Yes. Now that I know who it was back then... shit, I shouldn't have given up. That's why everything stopped for 10 years isn't it? He made me give up. I remember lying on my bed, chanting, 'Go away, go away...I give up.' Now though, at least I know to fight the feeling," he said, as the feelings associated with that night came flooding back and he was thoroughly angry at himself for being so spineless back then.

"Yes, fight it please," said Elizabeth, "Christ, he's referenced in everything from the Qur'an to the book of Enoch."

"So we know he's a big deal. And he's interested in us," Calvin said.

"You in particular," she said.

"Fan-fucking-tastic," he said, dripping in sarcasm. "Now to figure out why... I need to just keep reading, keep seeking. You must be something special Calvin. So why you, I wonder? What do you have that it wants?"

"Well, I know that it doesn't want you and me together. I know that had you been alone in the cemetery, it would have killed you. I snapped you out of whatever trance you were in and we got out of there. So it wants you too. Seamus told me this stuff, I meant to tell you..." he said.

"Jesus..." said Elizabeth, "Yeah, that would have been good to know! That explains why this day feels so ominous, and why things are getting weird."

She paused, then said, "Calvin, we've got something after us."

"I'm not afraid," he lied.

"Well I'm glad you're brave; it's refreshing. You know he's chief of the fallen angels, right?" Elizabeth said, with a hint of sarcasm.

"Most of the information on him in this book is in other languages, but so far I've gathered something about a lost human love... It's hard to know with the ancient ones. Just like history, they get diluted," she said.

Trying to show more bravery, he said, "We're just gonna have to call a meeting, and say 'Samael, get in here! We need to talk."

"Christ... no! Please don't say that. PLEASE don't say that. I just don't want it to come near me. To get... in me," she said.

"No... Christ no... I don't want that again."

"Just know, if you ask, if you summon, it will happen. Keep that in mind always," she said.

Calvin wanted to diffuse the situation with anything, and get off the topic of Samael.

"Elizabeth," he said, "What do you think of Sylvia Browne, James Van Praagh... people like that?"

"I detest them," she said quickly. "I think they give people with abilities bad names."

"Interesting. They were on CNN arguing with skeptics on how real 'psychics' are," he said.

She replied, "Who really charges 500 bucks an hour for a reading? Abilities are GIFTS. I mean, it's like charging someone to tell them to watch out for the truck that's coming their way, you know? When all it takes is... 'Hey Mister, there's a truck coming your way... pay attention!'"

Calvin laughed, then again changed the subject.

"Do regular people, people who aren't like us, have the ability to hear from spirits?"

"Of course. Everyone has abilities, some people are just more open to them," Elizabeth said.

"Cal, the more people who can do this, the better for the world," she said.

Hannah and Sterling were starting to get restless and Calvin ended the conversation with Elizabeth. His kids' squeals were a sure sign that he'd spent far too long on the phone and had better make them some lunch.

"Daddy, who were you talking to?" Sterling asked as he climbed into his seat at the kitchen island.

He looked at his son's big, curious blue eyes and smiled.

"Remember that nice lady who came over here and brought you the presents?"

Sterling nodded his head a few times.

"Well kiddo," he said, "I was talking to her."

"Why?"

"We have some things to do together."

"What kinds of things?" said Sterling. Evidently, Calvin wasn't going to get off easy. He spread jam onto bread for sandwiches and said, "Well, you know those bad dreams you've been having? We're going to try and make those go away for you."

"Ohhhhh, that would be really good Daddy. I don't like that man who comes," said Sterling.

"I know, Buddy."

Calvin didn't see it as just a bad dream anymore and wanted desperately to stop Samael, or whatever it was, from ever scaring his son again.

Chapter 14
A New Year
Saturday, December 31, 2005

Calvin looked forward to Saturday mornings. They were Lisa's morning to sleep in, which meant he had a couple of hours to himself. Sure, he had the kids, but they liked to start their day with TV, and he didn't complain.

This morning, Hannah was not feeling well; he figured she must have caught Lisa's illness, as she was listless and pale. He set her and Sterling up in front of the TV and got them some water and a bowl of cereal with their favorite soy milk. With the kids content, he went ahead and logged onto IM to chat with Elizabeth.

He waited as the messenger service signed him in. The chime of a new message told him Elizabeth was online and waiting. He reached for the speakers to turn off the audio, and hoped Lisa hadn't heard the chime. He was pleasantly surprised when he read the message.

To the moon...and back says:
Happy New Year to ye, ya arse

He hadn't expected this.

'They,' somehow, always seemed to know when he would have a few moments to talk. The fact that he was communicating with ancient spirits through the modern technology of Instant Messaging was incredibly ironic and still a little far-fetched and hard for him to believe, but he rolled with it. Plus, Seamus was becoming his favorite spirit to communicate with. He was crass and upfront, and Calvin admired that.

He typed back.

CALVIN says:
Happy New Year, Seamus!

To the moon...and back says:
Pick up yer balls youngin, you have a hell of a year ahead.

His heart pumped adrenaline through his body. He wasn't sure if having a hell of a year ahead was a good or bad thing...

CALVIN says:
And you're gonna help me through it, right?

To the moon...and back says:
Haven't failed one another yet.
Ye have a fair well of success.
Ye have love around ye.
Ye will come to know who ye are finally, you stupid arse.

It looked like this would be a good conversation. He liked the sound of coming to know who he was, though he thought he already had a pretty good idea.

To the moon...and back says:
Ye gotta work on that blockage though brother.
Remove yer shackles.

He wondered what blockage of which Seamus spoke. How could he remove something if he didn't know what it was? He waited for more information from Seamus on how to do it.

To the moon...and back says:
My dear saint and sinners I miss ale.
Are ye celebrating for me tonight brother?

Calvin laughed. This is why he liked Seamus so much, it was like talking to a guy friend, which he didn't have many of anymore. He wanted to say that he had something wild planned, and was going to drink the night away. He figured that's what Seamus wanted to hear, since he could no longer experience that part of living.

CALVIN says:
As much as I can I guess, with a sick child.

To the moon...and back says:
Aye.
So yer girl, the guardian...

Once again, he was caught off guard by the terminology. Was Seamus referencing his wife with the term guardian? Or possibly Elizabeth?

CALVIN says:
Do you mean my wife? A guardian?

To the moon...and back says:
Aye.
And there is love, no doubt.

CALVIN says:
What else do you know about her?

To the moon...and back says:
On a personal level git? Or on a spiritual plane?

He chuckled. He found it funny that Seamus would think he'd ask about his own wife on a personal level, when he had someone on the spiritual plane at his disposal. He found it ridiculous, actually.

CALVIN says:
spiritual, ye git.
See, I can do it too...

To the moon...and back says:
aye, 'bout fookin time.

He liked the way he swore, and could imagine how it sounded back in 13th century Ireland. Calvin wondered just how far back his spirit went. After all, Jade had said that Elizabeth and he were the oldest spirits currently alive...

CALVIN says:
So how old am I? Is my spirit?

To the moon...and back says:
How old can ye grasp?

CALVIN says:
Try me.

To the moon...and back says:
If we all come from the same energy, aren't we all relatively the same age?

He was disappointed with that answer, but figured it sounded like something a spirit would say. To his relief, Seamus wasn't done.

To the moon...and back says:
Ok, ok, I'm an arse.
In human concept of time ye lived many ages over.

He leaned in toward the screen.

To the moon...and back says:
The fall of Caesar, the crucifixion of Christ, the fookin theft of pagan life, the druid ages... all of those, go beyond that.

Calvin was quite pleased with the answer. But as usual, the more answers he received only led to more questions.

CALVIN says:

If so old, why haven't I found out who I am yet? Do we just get to the Earth and forget everything our spirits know?

To the moon...and back says:
Aye, at times we do.
But you, dear brother, pick an experience each time of learning and finding, exploring and saving.
Each life you perfect 'being' a little more.
You love that much deeper.
You don't usually settle, that's fer sure. That could be the cause of yer relationship trouble, ye arse.
If one thing is left half done, you will come back and experience it again until it's perfected. How do ye think ya got so ancient?

If he had any doubts about spirits coming back to life, this squashed them. It also made him seem like he was either a perfectionist or a terribly slow learner. He chose to believe that he was a perfectionist, and wanted to keep coming back to live a perfect life, to be the perfect man. And if he'd lived so many times, he surely had to be getting close! His attitude, arrogance and cockiness grew a little with that thought. He grinned to himself.

To the moon...and back says:
And don' be worryin' about yer home. It is safe, even if it doesn't feel like it at times.
Tell yer girl to not be afraid, love serves as a protection. Her love for you, yer love for the kids.
That son of yers protects ye more than ye know. It's an unbreakable circle of love, for as long as that love holds true...

Just keep askin' yerself this: Yer girl is a good woman, but is she your woman?

Calvin's smile broadened and, for the first time, he wondered about the very real possibility that Lisa wasn't his true love. Eventually he'd need to find a way to tell her, but now wasn't the time. He quickly signed off the computer as he heard her footsteps approaching from the hallway.

...

Calvin's phone rang at midnight.
"Who could that be?" Lisa asked. She grabbed her husband's phone and looked at the Caller ID. Calvin knew it would be Elizabeth, suddenly remembering that she'd call at midnight.
"Of course, it's Elizabeth," Lisa said with a defeated tone in her voice.
"Hello?" she answered. "Hi Elizabeth. Happy New Year to you too. Yes, we had fun. We are just at some friends' house. You want to say hi to Calvin?"
Lisa was obviously not happy at the intrusion, as once again this woman had come between them. Calvin tried not to seem too eager to have the phone passed to him.
"Hey Elizabeth! I'm glad you called," he said as he stepped out of the room. "I think we're going to have quite a year together."
"I think so too, Cal. As hard as things are right now, I'm glad we're going through it together," she said.

"Me too. Hey, any spiritual activity lately? It's been pretty neutral over here today," he said, not wanting to get into a long discussion on his conversation with Seamus earlier in the day.

"They usually try to give us a break when they know we need it," she replied, "Don't worry, it'll pick up again. And Calvin, just know that you can make this all stop. You can still give it all up, if it's too much, if it's too hard, if it's wreaking too much havoc in your life. Remember, the stars incline, they don't decide. You still have two weeks to give it up. You don't HAVE to do this…"

He quickly responded, "I do want this Elizabeth. And I won't give up."

With that, they said goodbye and he headed back into the room. Lisa had gathered the children and said it was time to go.

She was visibly upset.

Once in the car, Lisa began, "I didn't want to bring this up tonight," she began, "But I was hoping our year would start out happy and things would start to get better. Instead, what happens? Elizabeth calls, not 10 seconds into 2006, and you leap up to talk with her. I can't keep this up for long. I've told you that."

"I know Lisa, and I've told you that I'm going to need some space and your support until the 14th," he said.

"And then I am to assume that this is all going to slow down, so that it doesn't dominate our lives? Just two more weeks and then our lives are going to return to somewhat normal? God Calvin, you have trouble enough balancing work and home life. This has become like another full time job for you. And your family always seems to suffer the most. So I hope that the two of you are figuring this all out. What was so important that you had to step out of the room to talk to her? And that she had to call us at midnight? You have to set some boundaries here Calvin!"

They pulled the car into the garage, carried the kids to bed, and retreated to their bedroom to finish the conversation.

"Elizabeth and I didn't really talk about anything when she called. It was just a 'Happy New Year' call."
He didn't have a reason for stepping out of the room, at least not one that Lisa would find acceptable, so he hoped that she would just let it be. She didn't.

"Don't you see what I mean?" Lisa asked, "She just called to talk and you stepped out of the room to speak with her. She's starting to take you from me. I have to tell you, I feel abandoned. I don't feel loved or respected, and I don't feel like I'm on the pedestal a wife should be on. Honestly, I feel fourth in line. You have work, spirituality, Elizabeth, then me. I'm not sure where our kids stand in that equation. I can't continue to have that be the way things are. I won't do that. And God Calvin, I shouldn't have to tell you this!"

He thought for a moment, his anger rising.

He said sternly, "Lisa, she's not taking me from you. I'm not interested in her like that."

Saying those words felt like a lie. Truthfully, he was starting to wonder what life would be like with her. He continued, "We just have a lot to do, stuff you won't understand. I'm dealing with some scary shit, and I need to make it go away. You remember that night 10 years ago, the Night of Pitchfork Man? Remember the dagger in the window? THAT'S the spirit we're dealing with now."

He didn't intend on telling Lisa that until after the 14th, but figured she might as well know. And maybe scaring her a little would make her back off.

"How do you know that? What does it want?" she asked,

"I don't know yet. Look," he continued, "I need Elizabeth to figure out how to do that."

"Oh, you NEED her, do you?" she replied, obviously upset, "You don't understand how excluded from your life I feel! You are tearing us apart Calvin."

Then she uttered the words he never thought he'd hear her say. She held her thumb and index finger slightly apart and said, "I'm this close to being in a marriage that I don't want. You're changing, Calvin, and I don't like the person you are becoming."

The words made him freeze. But he made no effort to apologize to her or to comfort her.

His ego simply took over, and he said, "The person I'm becoming is who I'm supposed to be. Strong and confident, for once."

He switched off the light, and they both lied down facing away from each other. Calvin could hear her trying not to cry; her breath came fast and shallow. He knew she'd just lie there, eyes open, and eventually start spewing her thoughts. He wanted to get to sleep before that happened.

Calvin slowly breathed out, letting his body sink into the bed and feeling his mind teeter on the edge of consciousness. With one more deep breath, Calvin eased into sleep but not in the way he always had. Calvin's body slept peacefully, but he could see himself from the corner of the bedroom.

Standing in one spot but seeing himself in another would have been unnerving, had he been in possession of his body and able to feel his nerves. Instead, his spirit had separated from his body and he watched as his body below labored to breathe. The sound of his breath was hitched and he wondered if this is what it felt like to die.

Only instead of dying, his body spoke; in the lilt of an Irish accent.

"Is what you said, said in pure love?"

"Seamus?"

Lisa's voice was barely a whisper.

"Aye."

She cried, but kept herself together enough to speak. "I just love him so much. Yet I feel like he is slipping away...."

"Aye. Just know that his intentions are pure. And don't ye feel poorly over what ye feel in yer heart. People change in life, they grow, and sometimes they move on. That's okay," Seamus said slowly. Calvin's breathing sounded more labored.

"Seamus? What about Elizabeth? Can I trust her?" she asked.

"Her intent is pure of heart. Remember that each spirit always has free will," he said.

The conversation, while short, opened Calvin's eyes to Lisa's point of view.

"Seamus, thank you for coming," Lisa said.

"There is no thanks in love," Seamus said, "But aye, we know when ye be needin' some encouragin'. Say his name, he is drained."

Lisa quickly and urgently called his name.

"Calvin! Calvin!"

She shook his shoulder.

Calvin's intake of breath was again fast and sharp. He was sleepy, disoriented and vaguely aware of the conversation Lisa had just had.

"Calvin, you just channeled! It was Seamus," she said excitedly.

"I know... I think," his reply was groggy and half-aware.

"I do love you, with all of my heart. For better or for worse... I don't want to lose you."

She kissed him on the cheek and turned back over. An instant later his breathing was slow, deep, and familiarly all his own.

Chapter 15
Giving up?
Monday, January 2, 2006

Once again, Calvin arrived at work exhausted and drained. Arguments with his wife in addition to the spiritual happenings were taking their toll. He'd been surprised for weeks now that his work life wasn't suffering as a result, especially with all the time spent online with Elizabeth.

He opened his email though, and saw a message from his boss, Casey. It was short, and read, "We need to talk. Mable and I need to meet with you this morning. I'll be there at 8:30."

His heart sank and his stomach lurched. Mable was the owner and CEO of the company, and Casey was the president. Whatever this was about, it wasn't going to be good. Was he going to be fired? Were people complaining about his lack of contact with them or his complete lack of productivity during the workday?

Casey entered his office just a few minutes later. "Hey Calvinator," he said, "What's going on?"

Casey often used the nickname. It was weird at first but as they became friends it just kind of fit.

"Oh, not much," he replied.

"No, I mean with you. What's up?" Casey asked again. He and Casey had developed a bit of a friendship over the years, but it never evolved further than meeting for a few beers after work. Still, Casey was aware enough to know when Calvin wasn't being himself.

"Okay, you want the truth?" he said, "Lisa and I are going through some really hard times. Just last night she said she's not sure if she even wants this marriage anymore."

"I'll take her," Casey quickly replied.

He often made jokes like that, and never hid the fact that he thought Lisa was an attractive woman. Since Case was newly divorced, Calvin couldn't be sure just how serious he was. He smiled, and Casey continued, "Seriously man, if you need anything, let me know."

"Thanks dude, I appreciate it," he said, "Actually, you mentioned before going to see a counselor. Can you give me that name?"

Casey wrote the name of his counselor on a post-it, which Calvin slid into his pocket.

"I'll tell you what, I can even work it out so the company pays for the sessions, okay?"

He thanked his boss, then headed together into Mable's office and sat down in the throne-like chairs facing her massive art-deco desk.

"Oh, Calvin," Mable said.

He knew the tone. Just those two words seemed to say, "I like you enough as a person, but I'm not happy with you."

Just another demeaning woman in his life.

Mable was 65 years old, with short black hair and wore red round eyeglasses that were way too big for her head. The desk dwarfed her. She reminded him (and many others as well) of Edna from *The Incredibles*. He often kept this in mind when talking to her, providing himself with some comic relief as she tore into him for one reason or another.

Her office was an opulent display of 1920s décor. She spent thousands of dollars in design fees alone, not including the furniture. He hated it and never felt comfortable there. With the amount of money she spent on trivialities like her office decorations, this was a woman who cared for nothing except how much money was being deposited into her bank account. And that's what today's conversation was about.

"Have you looked at your P&L's lately?" she asked. In fact he did keep detailed records of his department's profit and loss.

"Yes, I have," he said confidently, "And I'm showing that our department is positive $70,000."

"Oh, that's weird, because I'm looking at the company records and they say you are negative $200,000. Maybe you just did your math wrong. What is your plan to fix it?" she asked in her condescending tone.

He began to fume inside, as her tone showed complete lack of trust in him.

"Mable, I don't have a plan to fix it. We're fine. I don't know what you are looking at, but I keep track of every cent coming in and going out of my production department," he said sternly.

"Hmm..." she uttered, looking directly at him. He stared back at her.

Casey took the opportunity to jump into the conversation, saying, "Calvin, take a second look at your numbers. We're a business, and that means all departments need to make money. We also need to talk about the performance of your TV spots lately. Frankly they suck. I need you to devote yourself, do whatever you need to do to get them back where they were. We need better spots and we need to spend less money creating them. Do whatever it takes. Work until 9 at night. Lie to whomever you need to lie to. Just get it done."

That didn't sit well with him at all. He knew he wasn't going to work 14-hour days, and he sure as hell wasn't going to stoop to lying to people who trusted him. But, he couldn't afford to lose this job right now; it paid too well.

He just nodded and said, "Okay, I will."

As they left the office Mable said in the same condescending tone, "Oh, and Calvin, I need to see your revised numbers. This afternoon isn't too hard for you, is it?"

"No Mable, I'll get them to you," he replied, defeated. After saying goodbye to Casey, he headed back into his office. He was pissed at the lack of trust displayed toward him. As one of the top five supervisors in the 100-employee company, he didn't feel like anyone other than Casey thought he deserved to be there. And while his pay was good, it was still less than what the other four supervisors received.

The rest of the morning was spent being yelled at by two of those supervisors, blaming him for mistakes they thought his department made. He was able to provide proof, after many phone calls and a couple of hours searching through his detailed records, that in fact the mistakes were the fault of the other supervisors. He was nearly ready to explode.

He'd had days like this before, always thinking it would get better. It only seemed to be getting worse. He had a bit of an epiphany, realizing that the majority of his co-workers viewed this job as their entire life. Most were single, and the majority of them had been divorced. He, on the other hand, was beginning to view his work not as his life, but as a way to afford *living* his life. He did see a potential divorce in his future though, and that was a scary thought.

Feeling defeated, drained and angry, he thought he'd better look at his P&L numbers and once again prove himself right. Then an email popped up in his inbox. The email listed no sender.

The spot where the sender's name should have been was completely blank. The subject line contained a simple period and nothing more.

He clicked to open the email.

Salut! It is my turn now. So now I have to wait in line to speak to my child?

He knew right away this wasn't an average e-mail. But who was it from? He read on.

I hope you know I joke with you. I am glad to be waiting. I am always glad to be there.

It didn't sound like Seamus, Jade, or Ellis. Who would say, 'Salut?'

Hard times all around I see? To be expected. They will try and break you. When you ask them 'Ce curu' meu vrei?' which is roughly meaning 'what the fuck do you want?' they tell you through their actions and through making life hard.

Seneda. Of course. He was mystified by two things: The fact that she was using what appeared to be Romanian, and that up until now his communication had been through IM with Elizabeth. Then he thought about the fax, and remembered Ellis saying how she sent it. "Channels," she had said, "Simply find the one going to where you want."
He didn't see why that wouldn't work for email too.
Calvin briefly wondered if anyone would ever believe that he was receiving messages from spirits through email.
He was also secretly amused that another email followed this one, from the company's IT guy that said the email server unexpectedly went down for a few minutes. It all seemed way too far fetched to be believed by anyone. Not that he planned on sharing his story any time soon.
He read on.

"Intreaba si ti va raspunde, kindred. 'Ask and you will be answered.' You say to them this, my son, you say, 'Pupa-m-ai in cur,' which is meaning 'kiss my ass.'

He figured that by 'they,' she was referring to Samael and whichever spirits were with him. Or maybe just his obnoxious coworkers. He was unsure which was worse at this point.

"a iubi, 'love each other.' Vi a forta, 'have strength.' They will try and corrupt your roots. You see it now, yes? Do not neglect that. You must make them happy in order for you to be happy in all areas.

Reading this made him think that Samael was getting to him, corrupting him, making him forget about love. But, had he ever known true love? Was Lisa his true love? Or was she simply a comfort and a stable part of his life? There's no way he could answer those questions right now. He kept reading.

"She tells you that you that you have two weeks, until ianuarie patruprezece, 'January 14,' and that it has to be de buna voie, 'of your own free will.' She gives you the option of leaving and giving up forever. I give you the option that I will beat you with my stick if you do. Ask Jack about my stick. It is big and leaves marks. I hope you know again I joke. But I do not joke about severity of this night, the level of commitment and dedication. Come only in having with you absolute trust and love and if you are having the feeling that it is something you want more than anything and forever. Keeping in mind that this being the night you commit to another experience and life. It is done once an existence.

Is this something Calvin wanted for the rest of his life? Maybe giving up would be easier, and just going back to the life he'd always known.

As difficult as life was right now, he couldn't imagine going back to how things were. He was starting to realize he LIKED the way things were going, and loved how his feeling of being different from others was finally starting to validate itself. In a sick way, he was enjoying his life of chaos.

Buna Noapte, my son. 'Good night.' Worry not for having me here. I come in dream and part there. Sunt de partea ta totdeauna, 'I am with you always.'

That was the end. This was a message he needed this afternoon, and helped him put into perspective the daily trivialities of his career. He suddenly didn't care if his bosses thought he lost nearly 200,000 dollars or if his moronic commercials weren't performing. He had a demon to deal with, and frankly, avoiding death was more important than office politics.
He forwarded the message on to Elizabeth, thinking she would be interested in reading it.
Her reply came a few minutes later:
"Wow, the way it's written...the English is so broken. I wonder if that's the way it sounds when she speaks through me? After reading this I believe we should go somewhere before the 14th. There's another cemetery I've wanted you to see. You have to understand the paths of the dark ones before you can revel in the light. How's your Wednesday morning look before work? Let's meet at the Greenwood Cemetery at six a.m."

He was actually excited. He thought of an excuse to tell Lisa right away. Since so many of his clients were on the east coast, he'd just tell her he had a conference call at 9 a.m. Eastern Time. He dialed Elizabeth's cell to tell her.

"Well that was fast!" she said as she answered her phone.

"Hi miss Elizabeth! Yeah, I can meet on Wednesday morning. Want to meet at the gates?" he asked.

"Let's actually meet a few blocks away and drive in together, in one car. It'll be easier to show you around. Cal, you know what happened at the Moran Prairie Cemetery? That's not even a 'dark' cemetery. Greenwood is. I just say that to prepare you. But I'll do a protective spell for us."

"A protective spell?" he asked, "You do spells?"

He was a little taken aback, as he hadn't heard her use that term yet. Calvin's preconceived notions of spells and witches were like anyone else's, and he had a hard time imagining Elizabeth in front of a boiling cauldron.

"Only when I need to. Remember what Jade said about magic? It's real. And we'll need to repel... him... the best we can."

"Okay Elizabeth, I trust you. See you at six on Wednesday."

"Good. Hey Calvin, How are you?" she asked.

"I'm fine. And you?" he replied.

"No, I mean it. No bullshit. How ARE you?" she asked again, obviously wanting more information than he gave.

"Okay, fair enough... Lisa and I... Honestly Elizabeth, at this point, I don't know what our future holds. We argued and argued the other night. She doesn't get it. She's feeling excluded. She says I'm tearing us apart. And you know, I honestly feel I need her to support me right now and to trust that things will even out. She asked what you and I do and what we talk about when we're together. I don't WANT to tell her everything for one thing. Plus, I don't remember everything! Now she feels like I'm not including her or loving her or treating her with respect. I'm to the point where I feel like I'm doing all I can, and if she doesn't get it, well, I can't control her free will..." Elizabeth sat silent for a few seconds, taking in his words.

"Wow," she finally said, "Jack and I had the same fight after I called you on New Years. Like exact, to the word. How odd."

"Jesus, that is weird. Looks like we're even going through our relationship problems together."

"Well, like Seneda said to you, there are hard times all around. We have to trust in love Calvin, in whatever, or whomever, our true love might be..." she said.

"Yeah, I guess that's another thing we need to figure out," he said. He couldn't deny his feelings for her, but wasn't ready to tell her.

Instead Calvin told Elizabeth something he didn't intend on telling her.

"Elizabeth," he started, "Lisa called on my way to work this morning, and asked if I was glad to get her call. I didn't answer. We just kinda sat there in silence, and then hung up. That's it. It was weird. We had NOTHING to say to each other. So I guess my question is, what the hell part of this is caused by a demon and what is just a pure lack of love?"

"Is there a difference?" Elizabeth replied, "If there's a lack of true love, does it matter if it's caused by a demon or our own lies? The cause is irrelevant. The question is, is it your truth?"

"I don't know that yet. We need the 14th to come, so we can just stop this thing and see if we can get back to some sense of normalcy. And then we can figure out where our true love lies... "

"I agree! Okay mister, I've got to run. See you Wednesday."

He closed his phone, quickly put some numbers together for Mable that he figured would pacify her, and stuck them in her inbox on his way out the door to pick up the kids.

When he arrived home, he was surprised to see Lisa already there. She was standing with her back toward him, reading something on the counter.

"Hey," he said, "What are you doing home?"

"My last patient cancelled. Thought I'd just come straight home and have you still get the kids. I went downstairs and stumbled across this."

She gestured to a large Bible open in front of her. She quickly added, "I haven't looked at it since we got it for our wedding, except to move it with us from place to place. I just went downstairs and started looking at the bookcase..." Her voice trailed off as she fell into thought.

He approached her from behind and looked at the cream-colored hardbound book. Lisa's godparents had given them the Bible, which Calvin found damn near insulting.

Anything having to do with religion raised his ire. He'd forgotten they even *had* a Bible stored downstairs on the bookcase. If he'd remembered he wouldn't have put it past himself to burn it just for the satisfaction of knowing how many people would be mortally offended. He couldn't hide the irritation on his face.

"I just had an urge to go get it Calvin," she said, "Maybe it can help, okay?"

She shut the Bible and turned to begin preparing dinner. He looked down at the closed book on the counter, and his jaw dropped.

"Holy shit...N-A-B..." he said aloud, astonished. The letters were still fresh in his mind since he saw them in the candle on Christmas night.

The letters were positioned on the spine of the Bible just as he had seen them in the flame of the candle. The words "New American Bible" were written on the cover.

Then he remembered the image in the candle flame that followed the letters.

"Lisa, there's a story in this one about a burning shrub or something, right?"

"It's in EVERY Bible, Cal. The Burning Bush." she said shortly.

"I had a vision on Christmas, while you were in the bath, with the letters N-A-B and an image of a burning bush. Do you know where that story would be?" he asked as he opened the Bible in search of an index or Table of Contents, not finding either.

"See, maybe there IS something to the Bible, if 'they' want you to read it!" she said happily.

"How are people supposed to find what they're looking for in these fucking things?" he asked as he flipped through the pages.

Calvin resorted to a modern search method: Google. He found the heading and then flipped pages until he found it.

"Here we go, Exodus 3, the Burning Bush..." he said. He began reading and summarized to Lisa aloud as he read.

"So Moses saw a bush that appeared to be on fire. A figure appeared in that fire... Jeez Lisa, that actually doesn't sound so far fetched anymore, does it?"

He continued, "Okay, so Moses walked over to the bush and the figure of God appeared in the fire. God said he's seen the suffering of his people and has come to help, and wants Moses to help him. Moses then asked 'why me?'

Calvin kept going, "Moses is concerned that no one will believe that God actually sent him. God says not to worry, that he'll always be with Moses. Moses says, 'Yeah, but what do I tell them? If they ask me your name, what do I say?'

"Oh, this is interesting. It says that God answered, 'This is what you shall tell them: I AM sent me to you.'

"Wow, he doesn't even call himself God in here, he just refers to himself as 'the God of your fathers.' I wonder if 'God' is just a name humans gave him?" He read the rest silently, before speaking to Lisa again.

"And basically the rest of the story is Moses being unsure about himself, being afraid of what people will think of him for making the claim that God spoke to him and God saying he'll give him signs and be with him."

"Fascinating..." he said.

"What do you think it means?" Lisa asked

"I don't know. Maybe it's just another piece of proof to help me stop doubting. I don't think this has anything to do with God though! I still have my doubts that a God even exists."

"Calvin are you that much of a moron? You know there are spirits now," Lisa said, "doesn't it make sense that there would be someone in charge of them all? Call that spirit whatever you want, but I think they showed you this so would believe in a higher power."

"I don't know. I can't jump to conclusions like that," he said, "All I can do is take this a step at a time and put pieces together as I get them. And hope that at some point, the pieces show a clear answer. I do find it fascinating that after being unopened for eight years you happened to get an urge to read the Bible, just days after that vision."

"Well, someone's obviously trying to tell you something, maybe they're using me to get to you too," Lisa said, looking a little more optimistic about her role in his life.

He nodded, then said, "Oh, Lisa, I almost forgot. Tomorrow morning I have to be in my office by six, for a call at nine Eastern."

Lisa didn't question his lie for a second.

This is getting easy...

...

Wednesday January 5, 2005

Calvin arrived ten minutes early at the deserted parking lot, just blocks from the gates of the cemetery. The sun had yet to rise and the cold morning air seeped into his car after he turned off the engine. Shivering, he started the Audi's engine again, turned the heat up to high and closed his eyes. Elizabeth arrived about five minutes after six. Not bad, considering she was over two hours late the last time they went to a cemetery. He smiled as she pulled her car next to his and got out. He unlocked the passenger side door for her, and she sat down with a sigh. She looked at him with a sparking smile and said, "Good morning... are you ready?"

Her feminine scent filled the car and he took a long satisfying breath. Breathing her in had a calming effect on his soul. He nodded, indicating that he was ready, then put the car into first and headed toward the gates.

"The gates are open... I was hoping!" she said, "They're ready for us."

Just past the gates were the cemetery's main offices. He could see a glowing lamp through a window, and wondered if they'd be bothered for entering before sunrise. This cemetery was much larger than the first, with three tiers of plots on the side of a hill; the lower level, a mid level, and the upper level. Thin winding roads connecting the tiers. The oldest section appeared to be in the middle, and Elizabeth gave him directions on getting there.

"Take a left here," she said.

There was still no sign of sunlight this morning, and the headstones appeared jagged and dark set against the black landscape. He couldn't see any dates on the headstones, but figured them to be around 100 years old.

"Stop here," Elizabeth said, "I want you to just sit. Watch and listen. Tell me if you see anything."

He looked out the driver side window, his heart beginning to pick up its pace as he realized he was sitting in a silent, dark, cold, and dead cemetery. He didn't see anything out of the ordinary. He looked ahead, taking note of the way the branches from the rows of old oak trees framed the eerily still cemetery. He found himself examining the beautiful, serene scenery more than searching for spirit activity.

"Calvin... do you see her?" Elizabeth said, interrupting his thought process.

"No, who?"

"There's a spirit approaching the car from my side. She's wispy, pale white. You don't see her?"

"I do..."

The spirit approached and peered into the car window, her hands shielding her eyes like a human would do when trying to look through a glass window.

"It's like she's trying to get a good look at who's in here..." Elizabeth said quietly.

It moved toward the front of the car and crawled across the hood, its eyes locked on the car's occupants.

"Calvin..."

His head snapped up, as he tried to determine where the voice came from. It was definitely not Elizabeth, so he attributed it to the specter outside.

"Calvin... come play with us...."

It sounded like a female child, the speaking was slow and deliberate. Drawn out, almost like it was taunting him.

"Who are you?" he said aloud.

"Why don't you want to come play with us?"

He was scared. It sounded like it could be the voice of an 8-year-old girl, but it was not friendly.

"Us? How many of you are there?"

"Come find out! We're hiding.... Come find us Calvin..."

He could see movement out the driver side window.

"You see us... darting behind headstones... come find us..."

The voice became more taunting, more frightening.

"Please come play..." the voice said, before changing to a gravely much more frightening, urgent tone, "We want to taste you..."

He started to sweat. The playful tone was gone and this came more like a demand.

The voice continued.

"You're gonna get coooold...."

He threw a glance at Elizabeth, whose head was slumped toward her chest.

"You know he's here, don't you?"

Again, Calvin's heart seemed to skip a beat as he answered, "Yes."

"Then why don't you come find him?"

Calvin didn't reply. They obviously wanted him to exit the car, which he briefly considered so he could stand up to these things and prove that he wasn't giving up.

"Or... we'll go find him for you..."

"Calvin! You okay? Get out of here! Drive!" demanded Elizabeth, obviously coming out of her catatonic state.

He started the car, put it in gear and tore out of the old section, heading to the top tier of the cemetery. The sun began to rise and being on top of the cemetery, away from the suffocating darkness of the old section, felt much better. A 50-foot cross stood at the highest section and cast a comforting morning shadow.

"Did you hear them?" he asked Elizabeth.

"No," she answered, "I don't know what happened to me. What did you hear?"

"A child's voice, taunting me to get out of the car. What was that? Why children?" he asked as he continued telling her everything he heard.

Elizabeth kept her cool and helped him rationalize what happened.

"Well, think about it. What kind of voice do people automatically trust? What conveys innocence?" she asked.

"A child..."

"Well, they weren't children, that's for sure Calvin. Sam...he...it... wasn't able to get to us, I'm guessing because the protection spell worked. But you think that's going to stop him from sending others? Thank you for not getting out of the car. You said they wanted to taste you? Well, they wouldn't have stopped. I think you encountered Lilin... I'll explain more later. Let's get out of here."

On the way out of the cemetery, Elizabeth pointed out a roped-off section that was bathed in the first sunlight of the morning.

"There's something I want to show you up there," she said.

He stopped the car to look at the narrow strip of grass, blocked off by a rope, leading up to a gazebo. He would have never noticed it was there by just driving by. Elizabeth exited the car, slid around the rope, and headed up to it.

Calvin followed.

"There's a new grave," he said. "Why would there be a new grave right here, hidden from everything?"

"I'm guessing it's a ploy. Put here to make people think this is a new section. This gazebo... it has some stories. Some say it was used for sacrifices. I don't why it's here, but I do know there are some harrowing stories of people crossing this rope at night."

Elizabeth reached to the collar of her shirt to adjust the sweater she was wearing, and panicked. A bare chain hung around her neck. Calvin noticed the look of panic on her face as she pulled the chain out and held it.

"Is that... THE necklace?"

"Yes..." she answered, "No clasp... Oh my God... check your car."

They sprinted down the hill back toward the car. Calvin checked around the floor of the driver's side while Elizabeth took the passenger side.

"Oh thank God, here it is," she said, reaching into the cup holder to grab the Celtic pendant.

"Did you hear anything or see anything?" she asked.

"No... how could that happen?" he replied.

"I have no idea. But I'm SO locking this up," she said.

...

Calvin arrived at work a little before 8 o'clock, still shaken from the morning's events. He told himself he was done with cemeteries for a while. He knew there was a lot to talk about, and he was dying for an explanation of the child's voice. What did Elizabeth say? Lilin? Once again, he logged onto IM even before opening his work email. Elizabeth was already on. He wrote to her.

CALVIN says:
    Wow. How are you? I'm still shaking.

To the moon...and back says:
    I'm fine. I've been doing some research.

To the moon...and back says:
Lilin. They are daughters of Lilith.

Elizabeth answered his next question before he could even ask.

To the moon...and back says:
Lilith is the great mother.
The Goddess.
The highest of dark.
Some say she's pure evil,
Some say she's pure dark.
I say she encompasses it all

Calvin didn't know how to respond, so he just waited for more.

To the moon...and back says:

Her daughters are Lilin.
They lure.
They are mischievous.

Now seemed like a good time to respond, at least to let her know he was still reading what she was writing.

CALVIN says:
So... her daughters were there this morning?

To the moon...and back says:
Yes, but that wasn't who was calling to you.
It was Lamia...
Lamia is a beautiful woman who hangs in graveyards and lures men to their deaths. Some say she isn't supposed to be able to speak due to having a snake's tongue and only is able to hiss.

CALVIN says:
And SHE wanted me out to "play?"

To the moon...and back says:
Yes.
Probably used Lilin to distract you. The wispy spirit we saw.

He had to know...

CALVIN says:
Be honest. What might have happened if I would have gotten out of that car and walked around?

To the moon...and back says:

You could have been seriously harmed.

To the moon...and back says:
They were ready for us Calvin.

To the moon...and back says:
Lilin can harm you.
Lamia can kill you.

Kill? He had wondered how a spirit could actually kill. He'd found comfort over the last few days in that a spirit couldn't physically kill a human.

CALVIN says:
There's something I've been wondering. Spirits don't exist on the same plane as us, right? They don't have physical bodies. How can they hurt or even kill us?

To the moon...and back says:
Cal, let me explain this so you understand. What are spirits?

CALVIN says:
They're energy. Right?

To the moon...and back says
Right. And what's... lightning? It's energy too, right? Can lightning kill? It doesn't take much to stop a heart Cal. All they need is a strong enough will and the intent to hurt or kill.

That clicked, and while it made sense it also significantly raised his level of fear. He sat and pondered what Elizabeth had just said, then she got back to the conversation at hand.

To the moon...and back says:
So, if you had gotten out of the car, they could have taken you. Then they would've had the relic too, and that would leave me...for it. It wins, it gets what it wants. So we need to figure out exactly what it's trying to stop from happening, and why it wants us specifically. If something like that is after us, we must be a fairly big deal!

CALVIN says:
Wow. So we're supposed to do something together that... it... doesn't want us to do. And we have a week to figure it out. Elizabeth, I've got to start paying some attention to work. I'll write later, K?

He signed out of the IM, somewhat ready to open his email and see what work crises awaited. He couldn't stop thinking about how easy it would be for his feeble human heart to be stopped. The messages piling up in his inbox seemed pretty pointless; there was the usual from clients, from employees, one from Casey, and one from Mable.
In the middle of them all was a blank email, looking just like the one from Seneda. The 'from' field was blank and the subject line included a simple period. Considering his mood, that's the one he opened first.

Anam Cara

Ye didn think I would let a mornin' like this one slide without speakin' to ye about it did ye?

Calvin breathed a sigh of relief in anticipation of some advice or reassuring words from Seamus this morning.

Aye, heavens no. Ye just keep sinkin deeper and closer to our foes and that is just fine a thing dear brother.
Ye won't get any 'gits' from me today.
Aye, the relic was ripped. Do ye not recall them warning it would get cold?
Well that would be the time them damned Lili distracted you and she was attacked. You turned just in time to make the pendant drop. Thank the stars. You'll have to ask her about her scratches tomorrow.

Calvin was upset with himself for not making the connection. And the scratches; he figured they'd look like the ones he got 10 years ago.

Ye, in all, a right brash mornin'. Enjoy yer time with yer family tonight brother. We are going to try and swing it so ye have a spirit free night. You need rest.

It was refreshing to see that Seamus was proud of him, and that he didn't come with more warnings of death. He wasn't sure he could handle any more of that.

Yer bein' so brave brother.
I know it's a hard time.
Just be steadfast and know yer stature isn't anything less than noble.

The way they spoke was so eloquent. "Your stature isn't anything less than noble." Who speaks like that?

Trust in love.
The trials this week won't be from just the darkness.
Strength takes braces from all sides

It was becoming a common theme to trust in love. He thought of his wife. No doubt he loved her, though he still questioned whether or not he was in love with her. He figured this experience would either prove that she's the one, or leave the door open to start something with Elizabeth. The thought excited him.

Ye were told ye had every choice.
Now is the time to start makin' those choices
Elizabeth has been ready for this coming week for some time.
Be the fookin' warrior you are, brother.
With trust and faith in the ancient ways I must away for now. But I'll be with ye, always.

"Be the fuckin' warrior you are."
The thought was in his head all day. It made him feel stronger as he dealt with the angry people who constantly blamed him for their mistakes. He simply didn't accept their negativity.
As messages from his guides tended to do, this one made him feel better and powered him through the rest of the workday.

...

He returned home exhausted and was useless in helping Lisa prepare dinner and in getting the kids ready for bed. He blamed his exhaustion on a long workday, which was mostly true, but was hesitant to tell her about the events at the cemetery that morning, which were the bigger factors in his fatigue. An internal battle raged as part of him clung to respect for his wife, while another part felt that things really weren't any of her business. It was a struggle that he felt daily, and it was yet another reason life lately was taking a toll on him.

Calvin felt like he was splitting in two; the old Calvin who settled for mediocrity, and this new one, who demanded to truly live and desperately wanted to experience true love.

Sensing the personal conflict in his head, Lisa looked at him, concerned and hesitantly asked, "Are you okay Calvin? You're looking... different lately."

"Like I said, it was a long day."

"I don't know if you're okay. Your eyes are sunken. You don't look at me the way you used to. You used to throw me loving and playful glances, but now all I see are angry and resentful glares. It scares me, and I don't know how to get my old Calvin back."

"Your old Calvin is just that... old. He's probably gone for good, Lisa. But let's focus on right now. Want to hear a story?"

"Fine. Okay," she replied.

"So, like everything else, this is going to sound really weird. But, I think it's interesting."

He had Lisa's attention, and kept talking.

"So Elizabeth's sister was visiting Ireland a few years back. While there, she stopped at an antique store and noticed an old necklace. She bought it and gave it to Elizabeth."

Lisa nodded and stared at Calvin intently.

"Well," he continued, "Check this out...evidently, I, in a past life obviously, got that same necklace for Elizabeth. A spirit came through and told us that. Isn't that amazing?"

It didn't occur to him that telling Lisa this story might not have been the best idea, because her reaction was one he didn't see coming.

"Jesus Calvin! Why the hell would you even tell me that? Are you trying to *make* me feel like shit or something? Do you *want* me to feel worse about this whole connection that you and Elizabeth seem to share, because I can tell you that I am already struggling with the entire thing on a daily basis as it is! You want to just pour salt in this wound?"

Tears gathered in the corners of her eyes, and rolled down her cheeks.

Calvin replied, "Whoa, what the hell? What do you even mean by that? I just thought it was incredibly cool that there was something that still existed from another lifetime! That it showed a connection from so long ago.... That's all."

He had no idea that this news would hurt Lisa so bad. "Why are you overreacting like this?"

"Oh okay Calvin. Do I really have to write this out for you? I already am having problems with how I feel about Elizabeth being thrust into our everyday existence. I feel that I have been a pretty supportive wife to you through all of this. I bet that any other woman in this situation would give her husband an ultimatum: 'Either she goes or I go.' But I haven't. I have let her into our home. I have not said too much about the excessive emails, instant messages, phone conversations... I have kept my mouth shut as I stress about how this has GOT to be affecting your job. I'm quiet about all that, and then you tell me that she has a necklace that you gave to her in a previous lifetime? How the fuck am I going to compete with that? One from ancient Ireland? What, did you go and make the necklace out of steel or whatever, forging it over a hot open flame for the love of your life?"

Calvin despised the childish sarcasm in her voice. Lisa continued, "Oh Elizabeth, how I love you! Let me make you a token of our love, that you can wear around your neck and have it hang close to your beating heart, so that with each beat you can think of the love that we share..."

Finishing her rant, she turned and stormed down the hallway.

Chapter 16
Murder
Tuesday, January 10, 2006

Elizabeth and Calvin hadn't seen each other in a few days and only four more loomed before the mysterious events of the 14th would unfold.

They planned to meet after work under the guise of another late commercial shoot. Calvin sat in his office catching up on work and waiting for Elizabeth to arrive at six. They didn't have an exact plan, just wanted to talk and see if they could put the puzzle pieces together and figure out exactly what they were supposed to do this coming Saturday.

His phone rang at 10 minutes till six.

"Hey, you coming?" Calvin answered.

"I'll be there. I stopped at the ATM to get some cash and the damn machine kept my card. I'll have to call the bank tomorrow. Just wanted to let you know that I'll be a few minutes late."

"That sucks. Did you enter a wrong PIN or something?"

"I didn't even get a chance!" Elizabeth replied, "I just stuck the card in and the screen said 'card confiscated.' There's nothing I could do. Anyway, not a huge deal. I'm excited to see you! I'll be there in 15 or so."

Calvin had given up on work a half hour ago, excited to delve into his 'second career,' as his wife called it. He debated on whether or not to tell Elizabeth about the burning bush story, deciding to hold off until the topic came up. Surely it was bound to when the time was right.

Just after six, Calvin headed downstairs to let Elizabeth in the main doors of the building. He glanced back at his desk, making sure he wasn't forgetting anything he needed to get back into his office suite. He grabbed his wallet but put his keys aside since he wasn't locking up.

Elizabeth's car wasn't parked along the meters yet, so he waited just inside the lobby where he could keep warm and watch for her. Within a minute, she turned the corner and pulled into an empty space in front of the building. He opened the doors for her and greeted her with a big hug before walking up the stairs to his second floor office.

"That's crazy about your card," he said as they turned the corner toward his office.

"Yeah, par for the course for me I guess, weird things like that are always happening," she replied.

He nodded and put his hand on the door handle to the suite and pushed. Nothing happened. He tried again, knowing he didn't lock the door. Again, the door didn't budge.

"It's locked."

"So unlock it, weirdo," Elizabeth said.

"I can't... the keys are on my desk."

Calvin was dumbstruck.

"How is this possibly locked? I left it unlocked so I wouldn't have to bring my keys. You can't even lock this door without a key, and the keys are inside!"

He was frustrated and confused.

"Just call the building maintenance people," said Elizabeth.

"Good thinking... The number is on the directory in the lobby."

They descended back down the stairs and he dialed the number, which went straight to voicemail. He left a message explaining the situation then folded his phone closed with a snap.

"Well, do you wanna go across the street and get a drink while we wait for a call back?"

"Sounds great! But I don't have a debit card or cash remember?" she said between giggles.

"I actually happened to grab my wallet before I left the office, just in case. I'm glad I did."

The bar across the street from the office building was mostly empty on the main floor, with no one up on the second floor. Elizabeth ordered a shot of whiskey, which surprised him. She didn't seem like a whiskey girl.

"It's for an old friend," she said, knowing what he was thinking.

Calvin ordered one as well and they headed upstairs for some seclusion.

They sat on the same side of a lone table that overlooked the main floor of the bar. Neither said anything, Calvin just sat there and took in her scent and admired her, thinking back to the first time he saw her and now being in a state of complete wonderment at all the events that have led them to this bar sitting next to each other.

Then he heard Elizabeth's voice; but with that familiar Irish accent.

"Brother, enjoy yer time with her tonight. But go back to yer office in 10 minutes. The janitor will be there to let ye in."

"Seamus!" he exclaimed, "Thanks. Hey, nice hearing your voice like this."

Until now, he had only heard from Seamus through the computer. Elizabeth's eyes were open, but distant and unfocused. He could see that Elizabeth was not there, which was more validation that Seamus was real.

"Ol' Samael sure doesn't want ye two together tonight does he? Now, ye git, are ye gonna tip back this shot o' whiskey with me or not?" Seamus asked. He smiled a broad grin and said, "Of course, brother."

He grabbed his shot and drank it at the same time Seamus did. Calvin's mind raced; so it was Samael who managed to make the ATM keep Elizabeth's card? And he somehow locked the office door, all in an effort to make it hard for them to get together tonight?

He's the king of the fallen angels and that's all he could muster?

Calvin laughed to himself.

"Hey Elizabeth!" he called to her, snapping her back, "We've got to get back to my office. The janitor will let us in."

"How do you know he'll even be there? Did you get a call?" she asked.

"An old friend told me," he said with a wink.

Elizabeth understood what had happened and followed him out of the bar.

...

Elizabeth had brought some small votive candles and pulled them out of her purse when they were finally alone in his office.

"They come to you better when there are candles, right?" Elizabeth said as she arranged them in a circle and lit each one. They sat across from each other, with the circle of white candles between them.

"Yeah, I do see them better when there are candles, thank you for remembering."

She smiled at him.

"Just let go, Cal. Find your Bahamas. This is a protective circle, so don't worry- no demons," she said with a grin, "Just let go..."

He sat cross-legged on his office floor. He focused on his breathing and letting his eyes adjust to the candlelight. He cleared his mind and let himself slip. As his vision blurred, a face slowly took shape.

She had a large, frying pan face with a wide nose and hair that appeared to be wrapped in a sort of bandana. She looked like a Romanian gypsy.

"Seneda!" he said, "I see you..."

"Yessssss," came the reply. Even that one word was said in a thick Romanian accent, and seemed to last a full five seconds.

She continued, "You see me... you feel me. I am always with you, my son."

There was a pause, like speaking took too much energy to continue. Her words were slow, as she seemed to deliberately choose each one.

"This story..." she said again, "This story you are living now...has potential... to be the greatest story..."

She paused again, before finishing her sentence.

"...Of all time."

He began to sweat. His heart beat faster, not able to comprehend what he'd just heard. The greatest story of all time? He couldn't believe it. It was turning into a radical, certainly unbelievable story, no doubt. But the greatest story of all time? He couldn't fathom it.

"Because of love," Seneda said again, "True... pure... love."

He just sat, taking in her words and trying to process them.

Seneda spoke again, "A request, my son. Tonight, when you see your son. Wake him if you must." Her voice became slower, and quieter, "Ask him tonight... and... every night... ask him what the favorite part... of his day was. His... *favorite*... part..."

Seneda seemed to know how Sterling would respond, as she grinned knowingly and slowly faded away. It was short, but he was sure he'd never forget these moments with Seneda and exactly what she said to him.

As she faded, the candle flame jumped. Elizabeth seemed to fall asleep, as she collapsed and slumped against the wall behind her. In the place that Seneda had just occupied, another being appeared. Calvin jumped backwards.

Samael was everything he'd imagined a demon would be: Its head wasn't human, but not animal. It had horns protruding from its head and wings arching from its human back. But it seemed weak, barely able to speak or even move. It leaned toward him, and took a few laborious crawling steps in his direction.

"Get out!" Calvin yelled, "You're not supposed to be here! Get the fuck out!"

Samael looked straight into him. Not *at* him, but directly into and through him. Its eyes were black slits.

It said in a slow menacing hiss, "I...am...not.....done with you....." and continued crawling slowly toward him.

Elizabeth suddenly became fully alert.

"Calvin! What's wrong? You look terrified!" she said, obviously scared. Samael disappeared.

"No, not terrified. Everything was so beautiful.... Until him. Samael was here Elizabeth. He said he's not done with me! Christ! You said this was a protective circle!"

"Well, obviously his magic is a little more powerful than mine!" Elizabeth shrieked.

"Yeah, obviously! Fuck..." Calving exclaimed, visibly shaken.

They both sat silent, trying to recover from, and comprehend, what had just happened.

Then Elizabeth spoke.

"Thank you for taking care of my best friend," she said.

He looked at Elizabeth and knew right away it wasn't Elizabeth speaking. His emotions let loose and he cried, as much from being nearly unable to comprehend the speed at which the spirits were coming and going as much as from the realization of who this spirit was.

"Ellis..."

"I'm happy with the sacrifice I made to bring you two together," she said.

He tried to hold back his tears, and said, "I'm so grateful for you, I love you... you mean so much to me."

"I love you too. And I reside with you. In your home," she said.

Her voice was confident, and not that different from Elizabeth's. He could tell she was a modern young woman rather than an ancient spirit. The fact that she was killed, sacrificed, as she put it, so he could meet Elizabeth twisted him up inside.

"That's beautiful, Ellis. You are so loved and welcome in my home."

"You know, if I was alive today, I'd sit you down and tell you that I'd rip your spleen out from your nose if you hurt her," said Ellis.

That made him laugh, yet pause. It was like a best friend lecturing the new boyfriend.

"Let's just sit and talk. I miss human interaction," she continued.

Calvin's thoughts went to how he could prove this conversation to Elizabeth later.

"What can I tell Elizabeth that only you and her would know?" he asked her.

Ellis paused, then said, "Tell her.. .chocolate milk. How anytime I was mad, or sad, she would come knocking on my door with chocolate milk and bridal magazines."

"That's pretty innocent for a couple of college girls, isn't it?" he said, amused by her choice.

"Those were some of the most ridiculous, funny times!" Ellis replied, "We laughed and laughed. Oh, and tell her about her sorority pin. She wonders what happened to it. I took it with me to Canada. It was with me when my body died."

He tried to take mental notes to remember all this to tell Elizabeth.

"Calvin, don't be afraid of death," Ellis said.

That snapped him back into the conversation, and he wanted to talk about her death. Her words also made him wonder if death was a distinctly possible outcome of this ordeal. His experience with Samael just now didn't comfort him.

"Do you know who killed you?"

"Yes. It was him," she said.

He knew whom she meant.

"Samael took over a homeless man, who was drunk out of his mind."

"Didn't he know that you would eventually bring Elizabeth and me together?"

Ellis responded, "He's powerful, but not that smart. He did it to hurt Elizabeth. Few things could hurt her more than taking away her best friend, right? Plus, he knew no spirit, except for him, had ever been able to get through to you directly. There's a reason, that you'll soon discover, why he hasn't been able to seriously hurt you yet though. Anyone else in the world he could take in a second if he wanted to. Not you two. So... to get to you, he'll first try the people you love. He hurts your loved ones, he kills your loved ones, and he begins to break you. Keep that in mind. And protect your family."

He thought of little Sterling's bad dreams again, and his rage toward Samael grew.

He had to wonder if Samael was able to get to Sterling because the circle of love in his home wasn't complete. Could it be that Lisa wasn't his true love? Was it Elizabeth? Could it be someone he hadn't met yet?

Ellis kept talking, "He knows who you are, even if you haven't figured it out yet. He thought he scared you enough 10 years ago to make you give up. And you did. Then he took me, as part of his plan to break Elizabeth too. But the consequence of that was a powerful love, a strong will and a pure intent... something he didn't foresee. I was able to use that to get through to you, and bring you and her together. Thanks for finally listening, moron."

"So let me get this straight," he said, "Ten years ago, Samael influenced me enough on the Night of Pitchfork Man to make me give up spiritual contact. So had he never killed you, you would have never gotten through to me, and none of the rest of all this would have ever happened. I wouldn't have met Elizabeth and I wouldn't even know that I'm supposed to somehow get rid of Samael. I wouldn't know he even exists! And he would have succeeded in his plan to keep us apart and to keep us from learning who we are..."

"That's right," Ellis responded, "Like I said, he's not smart. He doesn't understand the power of love. He got cocky. You'd given up, but she hadn't. He wasn't going to stop until she did. He didn't realize it, but his plan was complete 10 years ago. He let his own cockiness screw him over. But Calvin, this isn't done yet. Learn from his mistakes, okay?"

"Oh, and Elizabeth knows who she is now, and who you are," Ellis continued, "We had to give her that knowledge so she knew who to ask for help on the 14th. But I think she already knew. You're very special, Calvin. But don't let that go to your head..."

Her voice was trailing off as Elizabeth began to stir again. She managed to say one more thing:

"Because now you've seen how arrogance can lead to evil..."

...

Elizabeth's severe exhaustion showed in her face when she came to, her energy drained by the spiritual activity. Before they parted for the night, Calvin wanted to give her the messages Ellis left for her.

They sat on the fabric couch across from his desk, side by side as he explained everything, trying to get his words past the lump in his throat. When he mentioned the chocolate milk and bridal magazines, she laughed. When he got to the sorority pin, Elizabeth burst into tears. He wiped the tears from her cheeks as he finished talking, and waited for Elizabeth's reply.

She gained control over her sobs, and said, "You don't know what that means to me, Calvin. Thank you... I had given her my pin, just so she wouldn't forget me. I've been wondering if she still had it. The fact that she had it with her when she was..."

She couldn't finish her sentence, being overcome with grief all over again at the thought of her best friend's murder. The reality of human death took precedence over the novelty of spiritual contact. Tonight he saw Ellis as a human, as a person who had her life taken from her. She wasn't just a spirit helping them, she was Elizabeth's best friend. And she was dead.

"Elizabeth," he said, "I'm so sorry you lost her, I can't imagine. I wish I would have known her. But, I feel lucky to have her with us now. And you know that she's happy, and that she's with you."

Elizabeth looked at him and composed herself.

"I know. She was just such an incredible person, I loved her. I love her now. And she's going to help us take care of the sick spirit that killed her, once and for all. And, we're going to have a kind of help that you can't even imagine right now. We're going to be okay Calvin, we just have to get through until Saturday."
...

Calvin arrived home emotionally drained. Lisa was up waiting for him, and could tell that he'd been crying.
"What's wrong? Everything okay?" she asked.
He let loose, and told his wife about the conversation with Ellis. Lisa began crying too.
"She stays here, with us?" Lisa said, "That's amazing, I love it."
"It's incredible, isn't it? And the things she wanted me to tell Elizabeth meant so much to her... I've been crying all night."
He also told her about what Seneda had said, and remembered to go ask Sterling the question. When he opened his son's door, Sterling sat up, and said, "Hi Daddy."
"Hey kiddo," he said, sitting next to Sterling on his bed, "How was your day honey? I want to know what your very favorite part of the day was."
Sterling sat for a moment, then said, "Umm, right now. You coming home, Daddy."
The child wrapped his little arms around Calvin's shoulders and squeezed tight. Calvin hugged him back as another tear ran down his cheek.
"Goodnight my special little boy. Sleep well, okay?"

Sterling nodded, lied down, pulled his covers up to his chin and closed his eyes.

...

Wednesday January 11, 2006

"Oh thank God you answered," Elizabeth said, after dialing Calvin's number. "I've had the scariest, most horrifying morning of my life."
Calvin could hear her tears and desperately wanted to hold her, to comfort her. "My God, Elizabeth, what happened?"
She described her morning in detail.
"I was supposed to be at work by six a.m. because Grace's parents both needed to get into work early. I was running late, and didn't get out of my apartment until a quarter to six. The drive normally takes 20 minutes, and I had less than 15.
I turned onto the highway, a narrow two-lane road. I was speeding, maybe 15-over. It's raining, and I couldn't stop thinking about Ellis, and what I was going to do with Grace today. I was an emotional wreck, even before it all happened.
Out of the corner of my eye, I saw movement and slowed down. A huge buck, and I mean huge, with antlers and everything, shot out and then stopped, right in front of me. I closed my eyes and screamed, and slammed on the brakes. After I stopped, I opened my eyes, and it was still standing there, right in front of my car. It's so weird, I made eye contact with it, then it suddenly turned, looked toward an oncoming truck and sprinted directly into its path. God Calvin... I can't stop crying.

A little red pickup slammed head-on into that deer. I saw its head crash into the windshield then tumble off the side of the truck. The truck spun 180 degrees and stopped in a ditch on the side of the road. The buck was dead next to it.

"My God Elizabeth, I'm so sorry... Are you okay?"

"Physically yes, I'm fine," she replied, "But I sat sobbing in my car, not far from the truck. I didn't see any movement from inside. There was so much blood on the windshield, and I was too afraid to go check on the driver. I should have. I called 911 and waited until the ambulance came."

"You did the right thing, Elizabeth," Calvin said, "I'm so glad you're not hurt."

"Me too, but I think it was supposed to be me. I was supposed to hit that deer."

"I know sweetie, but it wasn't. I'm so glad you're okay."

"That's not even all," said Elizabeth. "I turned onto the dirt road that goes to Grace's driveway, still in shock. Again, out of the corner of my eye, I saw movement. I looked out the side window up the hill, and a massive pine tree slid off the ledge above the road, almost directly above me. I screamed, again, and slammed on my brakes just before the tree crashed down across the road. It just missed my car. Branches were on the hood!

"Where are you now? Are you safe?" Calvin replied.

"Yes, I'm at Grace's now, but after it happened I couldn't stand. I fell onto my knees and gasped for air. It was twice in less than 10 minutes that I could have died, and I know who was behind it. I don't know if I can do this. I think I'm crumbling, Calvin. I never asked for these abilities, and I don't think I want them anymore. I think I want out. I think I want to quit."

"No, please, Elizabeth, I need you. You're the strong one here, the one who doesn't quit. You know he's doing these things so you give up. Please... Ellis said you know things that I don't. About who you are, about who I am. Please don't leave me alone."

"You're right. I'm sorry. This is just so intense and I'm so ready for it to be over."

"It's almost done. Please stay strong."

"I need you Calvin. I couldn't do this without you."

"I need you too. Bad. We can get through this together. Hey, how'd you get past the tree and get to work?"

"I composed myself enough to call Grace's dad, and explain that a tree had fallen and was blocking my path. He and a few neighbors came out with chainsaws and cleared the road."

"I'm still shaking Calvin," she said, "And the man in the truck that hit the deer, I can't imagine he survived... I don't know if I can take it if people start getting hurt, when it's supposed to be me..."

"I don't really know what to say. I'm just so glad you're okay," Calvin said, "We just have to be really careful the next couple of days. I think he knows that it's now or never for him. Keep your eyes open Elizabeth, and I will too. Like they say, trust in love... right?"

....

Calvin couldn't get his thoughts off of Elizabeth all morning. His concern for her wellbeing outweighed his desire to get work done. At lunchtime he opened up IM and he sent her a message.

CALVIN says:
How are you doing?

To the moon...and back says:
Thank you for telling Lisa about me.

The response wasn't what he expected or had hoped for. He read Ellis's response again, and took some comfort in knowing that she was with Elizabeth. He took a deep breath and prepared for a conversation with Ellis.

To the moon...and back says:
I sat and listened and cried and laughed with you.
It was a good night for me.

CALVIN says:
It was a good night for me too.
Hey, stupid question, but what do you do where you are? What's it like?

To the moon...and back says:
I observe,
I learn,
I laugh,
I love,

What do you do?

He began to think that the biggest difference between being human and being spirit was just the whole breathing and having a body thing.

CALVIN says:
Wow. Much of the same, actually.
What about time passage? Is time the same here and there?

To the moon...and back says:
Time... you'll learn that time is truly relative

It was another generic answer that he couldn't really comprehend at the moment. He thought he'd bring up last night again instead.

CALVIN says:
Hey- you must have seen Elizabeth's response to the chocolate milk and the pin... meant the world to her.

To the moon...and back says:
I felt bad! Girlfriend busted out crying
Do you know that Elizabeth really never was a crier when we first met?
I love that she cries easily now. And you too, ass head.

CALVIN says:
I'm not a crier. I still hold to that.

Although he wasn't sure how he could even say that after the last 24 hours.

To the moon...and back says:
You can't hold to any of your old bullshit Calvin. Not anymore. The stakes are too big.

With that, Elizabeth's chat went offline and he had no choice but to go back to work and hope the 14th would come without further incident.

...

Friday January 13, 2006

Lisa woke Calvin up with talk about the necklace. Friday was her day off and normally she slept as Calvin got ready for work. Today though, she evidently had too much on her mind.
"The stress is taking a toll on me, Cal," she said, "And I can't help but think about that damn necklace, and wonder why you gave it to Elizabeth, even if it was in a past life."
Calvin, still half asleep, registered what she said but wasn't in a state to respond. She continued.
 "It has to prove that your connection must have been close; an intimate relationship that has spanned lifetimes. It's eating me up inside. I'm sad, to the core of who I am."
"And I can't help but wonder if you're falling for her, all over again."
Calvin, more awake now, grabbed her hand and gave it a reassuring squeeze, but only managed to say, "I've got to get up, I'm going to be late for work."
He called Elizabeth on his drive and told her about the morning talk.

"That's funny, I was thinking about her this morning and started writing an email to her. I think I'll tell her that we were siblings, that should ease her mind," Elizabeth said.

Calvin felt incredibly nervous at the thought of the woman he was developing feelings for emailing his wife, but he liked her idea and trusted her to not say anything rash. In truth, Calvin had to believe that he and Elizabeth were lovers, but he figured the email would work to ease Lisa's mind and he smiled, hoping tomorrow would come and go without incident.

Chapter 17
Scare Away the Dark
Saturday, January 14, 2006

Calvin awoke after a miserable night's sleep. The day had arrived, yet he still didn't know what he was supposed to do. He was nervous, scared, and anxious, yet excited to get this done and try to return to a more normal life. This was the day they would either succeed in destroying Samael or get destroyed trying.

He knew this newfound spirituality would be a part of his life for good, and living without the constant threat of a demon would be welcome. He was tired of the evil in his head and tired of feeling that sickening presence near him. What he did like however, and what he hadn't mentioned to anyone (even Elizabeth) was how powerful and invincible he felt lately. It seemed to grow with each passing day, even though each day tended to be more frightening than the last.

The last couple of days though had been surprisingly quiet. While it was a relief, it was also a cause for concern. Was Samael saving his energy for today? He sure hoped Elizabeth had a plan, because he didn't.

The thoughts taunted him through the night. He'd fall asleep for what seemed like moments only to jolt awake again by his raging mind. By five a.m. he startled awake one more time, this time to the familiar creak of his son's bedroom door. That was enough of an excuse to give up on sleeping and drag himself out of bed. He wanted to get this day started as normally as possible, because he was sure it wasn't going to end that way.

Elizabeth arrived at the house at 10 a.m. Calvin had asked her to come over before they headed out for the day so she could look at Sterling's bedroom, just to see what kind of feelings she got from it. Sterling and Calvin answered the door together.

"Hey Elizabeth," he said with a smile. The sight of her was enough to calm him down a little.

"Come on in."

Lisa came around the corner and uttered a slight gasp, presumably surprised by Elizabeth's appearance. It was a 180-degree shift from the first time they had met in this same doorway. Instead of her radiant smile, feminine clothes, and bright personality, Elizabeth came dressed in all black. A loose-fitting knee-length skirt hung from her hips, which she paired with a tight long-sleeved shirt. Even her face was done in an almost gothic style; black lipstick and dark eye shadow. Little Sterling noticed too.

He looked up at his mom and said, "Is that Elizabeth? Are you sure? The same Elizabeth we saw before? She's different."

Lisa was slightly embarrassed but knew he had a point.

Elizabeth bent down to his level and said, "It's me, Mr. Sterling. I know I look different today, but everything's okay, I promise."

That was enough to satisfy him and he turned from her and tore into the kitchen to finish his breakfast.

Lisa finally spoke, "Thanks for the email, Elizabeth. I'm so nervous for you guys today. Do you know how long you're going to be out?"

"I'm not sure," she replied, "We need to get some supplies then make a couple of stops. It'll probably be late afternoon or evening before we're back."

"Lisa," she continued, "Focus on your love for your kids today. I mean, really focus on it. There is no love stronger than the love between a parent and a child."

Lisa grinned. Focusing on her love for her kids wasn't a tall request.

"So, mister," she said, looking at Calvin, "I need to look at Sterling's room."

"Yeah. Just go in there and tell me what you feel, if anything," he said.

Lisa and Calvin followed Elizabeth to Sterling's room. She entered while they stood in the hallway. The room was a perfect little boy's room, with the walls painted blue, a multi colored ceiling fan, and a dark cherry wooden bed with a matching dresser. Elizabeth immediately turned toward the closet and quickly slammed shut the bi-fold doors. She stepped back from them, staring intently.

She then approached again, muttering something under her breath while she dropped to her knees and touched the trim where it met the carpet on the left side of the doors. She slowly traced her hand up the left side, stood on her tip-toes to slide her hand across the top trim, and all the way down the right side. Then she stood in the middle of the room, arms open to her sides, eyes closed and continued the chant-like muttering that neither Lisa nor Calvin could understand.

"Whew, that was powerful," she said.

"So there WAS something in there!?" Lisa exclaimed.

"I'll just say that he should sleep better now. And don't open those closet doors for 24 hours, please."

"You okay Lisa?" Calvin asked.

"I'm scared, and not feeling like I want to be left alone, especially knowing what you guys are going to go deal with today."

"Don't worry Lisa," Elizabeth said, "It's gone now. We just need to let the energy in there dissipate uninterrupted for a while."

Lisa nodded.

"Remember honey, love those kids today. You ready Cal?" Elizabeth said.

"I guess so," he said. He gave his wife a quick kiss, then followed Elizabeth out the door and into the torrential rain storm that had apparently started between the time Elizabeth arrived and when they left.

...

"So what was it?" Calvin asked.

Elizabeth knew he was referring to Sterling's bedroom.

"A helper, I'm guessing. Something 'it' put there to stand guard, to instill fear. Samael can't get into your house and hurt anyone, I'm sure it's protected by your guides. But that's not going to stop him from slipping someone else in and scaring the shit out of little Sterling. The more fear he can create, the more powerful he is," Elizabeth said.

Cal fumed.

"It's okay Cal, be angry. Be dark. Today, we let the dark take over. Feel the anger. We need it. He might feed off it, but today we need him to. That's why I kept telling Lisa to feel the love today. We need to balance our emotions with love, I can't stress enough the importance of balance."

Calvin didn't have any problem slipping into anger, especially with the motivation of protecting his son. The powerful, invincible feeling was back. He wasn't scared anymore, even of Samael. His eyes tightened into a squint. He could feel his dark hair, which he hadn't cut in at least two months, hanging into his eyes and over his ears, resting against the collar of his black jacket. He looked down at his hands, which were tightly clenched on his lap over his black jeans. Without even realizing it, he had dressed in all black as well.

Their first stop was at the old flour mill in downtown Spokane, which had been converted into a collection of eclectic little shops. Elizabeth explained that one of those shops was where she preferred to get supplies. Standing in the short checkout line with black candles, a lighter, and a container of sea salt, Elizabeth noticed a line of demon heads hung on the wall above them. They were the type of gargoyle-type decorations that young angst-ridden teens hang in their rooms. He shuddered when he saw the one that looked just like the demon that they were trying to destroy. Elizabeth noticed it too, and gave him a nod.

"The signs of him are all over the place," Elizabeth said after they were back in the dry comfort of his Audi.

"Things will really begin to change if we're successful today."

He didn't like that she had chosen the word "if," but didn't say anything.

"Then let's get this party started," he said, full of confidence.

"That's what I like to hear!" Elizabeth said, "Head down toward Grace's house. But don't turn on their street, keep going until the highway ends in a T."

He obeyed and drove.

"If my information is correct, it's just on the left side after we turn," Elizabeth said as they turned left at the T in the road.

"Yeah! Right there. Turn left through those gates."

Calvin had to slam on his breaks to avoid missing the turn into the narrow, weed-filled entrance he would have never even seen.

"What is this place?" he asked, trying to make out their surroundings through the rain soaked windows. "Those gates almost look like gates to a..."

"Cemetery. Yes," Elizabeth spoke for him, "This is an abandoned cemetery."

Sure enough, he could see toppled headstones through the overgrown weeds.

"This is the place he's been calling home... it's perfect for him. No one ever comes here, there's no disruption of energy, and plus, there's lots of forgotten spirits at his disposal. It's just like it looked in my dream..."

"So that's how you knew about this place..." he said. Elizabeth grinned, and said, "Along with a little inside information from some powerful people in the know."

She winked at him.

"You ready?" she asked as she gathered the candles and salt.

"So we have to go out there, huh?" he said, referencing the torrential rain as much as the cemetery itself.

"Yup. No more protection," she answered in a way that spoke to both of his concerns.

They opened the doors of the car and stepped into the saturated cemetery. His shoes sunk into a puddle of mud and the rain immediately soaked his hair. The cold penetrated his coat and he shivered.

Elizabeth, nearly oblivious to the rain, had already moved a few steps ahead of him. Calvin followed, admiring her courage.

By the time he caught up, she was busy arranging the candles into a circle.

"Hurry," she said, "Help me. Put these candles over there to complete the circle. Then stand in the middle of it with me."

"We'll never get candles lit in this rain," he said, assuming that was her intent.

"He's good isn't he? Notice the blue skies when you woke up this morning? We're in his home and he doesn't want us here. He's watching us now and yes, we're lighting these candles," she said in a determined voice as she ignited the lighter.

Calvin instinctively looked up into the trees and saw a dark shadow perched near the top of one of the old pines.

"Why doesn't he just attack if we're here without protection? I wouldn't even know how to defend myself against that!"

He had to yell in an attempt to be heard over the wind, which began to howl.

"The two of us together are more powerful than him. And you've got protection that you can't even fathom right now. You'll see later. Now, light these damn candles. We need to neutralize this place and get him out of here. Magic, Cal. It's real."

Elizabeth managed to get one of the candles in the circle lit, but by the time she attempted to light the next it was extinguished by the rain.

"Cal, I need you," she yelled, "Use your will and intent. We NEED these candles lit. Do NOT let them go out, okay? Tell them if you need to. Actually use your voice, point to them, and DEMAND they stay lit, okay!?"

Elizabeth lit a candle, its flame dancing and flickering as the rain pounded it. The flame again extinguished. Elizabeth looked back at him and just said, "Relight it."

"But I don't have a lighter."

"I just told you Calvin! Will and intent! Use it, you don't need a lighter!"

He pointed to the candle letting the anger and confidence build inside him. He thought about his guides, about Sterling, about his dreams. He thought about the pagan warrior and vampire roots in his spirit.

He looked straight down his outstretched arm at the candle, which seemed to sit at the tip of his rain-soaked finger.

"Stay lit..." he growled as he focused every bit of intent he could on the candle.

The flame flickered back from nowhere and came back to life.

"Yeah!" he yelled.

Elizabeth had the second candle lit, and went toward the third. He focused all his attention, all his energy on keeping the candles lit as Elizabeth completed the circle.

"I've got them all. You keep them going while I do this spell!" she yelled at him. His attention was fully on the candles, and he barely heard what Elizabeth was saying. She threw the sea salt in each direction; East, South, West and North while chanting something about each direction.

The raindrops grew larger, and as one candle flickered back to life another went dark. He spun in circles furiously keeping them lit with nothing but his finger.

"I'm done," Elizabeth said, "You can let them go out now."

He stopped, dropping his hands to his sides and exhaling hard. He could feel his hair flat against his face. He panted hard and the candles fizzled out within a few seconds. A few moments later the rain let up. He glanced back up toward the pine tree, and the shadowy figure was gone.

Could that have been it?

"He's not gone for good, Cal," Elizabeth said, with her hand on his shoulder, "He just can't be here anymore."

"Hey," she continued, nudging him and smiling now, "Still believe you can't do magic? That was incredible!"

She wrapped her arms around his neck and squeezed him close to her. He held his hands up with Elizabeth still hugging him and shook his head in disbelief, but smiled triumphantly. He hugged Elizabeth hard, pulling her tight against his body and relished in the small victory while taking in her calming scent.

They made their way back to the car, where Calvin briefly wondered about the effect of their sopping clothes on his brand new seats. The thought seemed so trivial now. He opened Elizabeth's door and held her hand as she collapsed into the seat before circling the car to get into the driver's side.

"So..." Calvin started, still bewildered at the events that just unfolded, "What just happened? Why can't he be there anymore? I don't understand."

"Some things are beyond our understanding," Elizabeth replied. "We need him to come to us later, and not just hide out here, biding his time."

"Can't he just bide his time elsewhere?" Calvin asked.

"Sure, but this has been his home base, so to speak, for who knows how long. It's like he's been kicked out of his home and is displaced. You should understand a little better by tonight. Things are about to get interesting..."

"Before we drive out of here," she continued, "There's one more thing we need to do."

Calvin's heart skipped a beat.

"We need to invoke some spirits who might be able to help us. Our next stop is the one where we try to banish him for good. And we're going to need all the help we can get. What I want you to do is invoke the spirit of anyone you think can help, okay? Just say, 'I invoke the spirit of..' and say his or her name."

Calvin paused, slightly relieved, but not knowing whom to mention.

"Oh come on, you have lots of spirit friends now, right? Invoke them, loud and strong."

"Oh, right!" he finally said, feeling like an idiot for not thinking of them right away.

"I invoke the spirit of Jade.

I invoke the spirit of Ellis.

I invoke the spirit of Seneda.

And...

I invoke the spirit of Seamus."

Calvin sat silent for a moment before continuing, "I don't know exactly what to say here, but we need your support. We need your love. Be our light as we scare away the dark. Just, please, don't let me fail. I need you. I need your help."

"Very good!" Elizabeth said, "Now, I want you to invoke two more. Him and Her. Just do it. Trust me."

Calvin looked at her hoping for more of an explanation. It was obviously not coming.

"Not yet..." Elizabeth said, reading his mind.

"Okay..." he replied and followed her direction.

"Thank you," Elizabeth said. "Now, drive to your office."

He wasn't surprised that this would all end in his office. It was quiet there, they could lock themselves in and be assured that they wouldn't be interrupted; especially with today being a Saturday. He occasionally heard of an employee coming in on the weekend to finish some things up, and hoped that wasn't the case today.

The parking lot at his downtown office building sat empty, which was a good sign. They entered the building and climbed the stairs to the second floor.

"The lights are off, that's good," Calvin said as he breathed a sigh of relief. He stepped out of the elevator and looked toward his office.

He hesitantly unlocked the door, they entered, and he locked it again securely behind them.

"That should buy us a few seconds anyway, if someone decides to come," he said.

"I don't think we'll be bothered," Elizabeth said, "At least not by humans!"

Calvin laughed.

"Okay," Elizabeth said, "Let's get prepared. We need to make another circle with the candles. A big one, around the perimeter of your office."

Elizabeth pulled more unused candles out of her bag; six black tapers and six black votives. They positioned the candles to alternate, one big, one small, in a circle. Elizabeth lit them all while Calvin stood in the center and watched. With all the candles lit, they stood inside the circle across from each other as the small flames cast a flickering orange glow.

"Again, there is no protection here. This isn't a circle of protection to banish the evil from coming like we've always done. This time we invite it. Are you ready? Be angry. Let him feel the hate you harbor toward him. Be strong. Invoke Samael."

Calvin's hands shook.

"What do we do when he comes?" he asked, beginning to panic.

"Just do it Calvin. We need him here," she replied.

He wanted to keep stalling. Now that the actual moment had arrived, he was scared out of his mind. His heart pounded like never before. His hands began to shake. He flashed back to the few times he'd seen the terrifying beast that was Samael. He remembered Elizabeth's reaction when he jokingly said he wanted to 'call a meeting' with him. He remembered the times at the cemeteries. He was losing faith in himself.

"I can't! I don't know what to do when he comes!"

"Do it! Remember how strong your will and intent were when keeping those candles lit? Use that same energy. Invoke Samael."

Calvin was impressed at her courage. Considering how scared she was of Samael when she first heard his name, he figured she must know what she's doing this time.

He took a deep breath that quivered in his chest, and thought about Sterling's nightmares again. He thought about the deer and the tree incidents a couple of days ago. He thought of the Night of Pitchfork Man 10 years ago, the first night he felt like he had something after him. This was his time to get revenge on all of that, and put an end to any more of it from happening in the future. This was for his son.
"I invoke the spirit of Samael,"
It came out as more of a guttural snarl than a demand.
He stood with his fists clenched, his jaw tight. He looked around the room, looking for any sign of Samael.
"Is he here?" he asked Elizabeth.
"Do you feel him?" Elizabeth replied in a slightly sarcastic tone.
"Invoke him again."
Calvin's anger grew as he said, "I invoke the spirit of Samael!"
Still, nothing.
...
"Why isn't he here?" Calvin asked.
Elizabeth didn't respond.
He looked toward her only to see her now-familiar yet awkward lifeless pose; she sat on the floor, legs criss crossed, shoulders slumped forward and her head hanging above her knees. He looked around the room and noticed the candle flames beginning to dance, their flames joining into a single light formed over the candles, and congregating over Elizabeth's head in a single ball of flame, light, and energy. He saw a face, similar to what he saw in the candle flame on Christmas night but on a much larger scale.

It couldn't be Samael... or was it?

Then he heard a voice. Male, powerful and strong. Unmistakably this was the voice he heard on the Night of Pitchfork Man that told him not to turn down his usual street. It was just one word but it was unforgettable.

"Do you know how many humans have successfully been able to invoke me?"

It had to be him, even though it didn't feel right.

"You are done!" Calvin awkwardly yelled, "You are not getting out of this room!"

His threats fell embarrassingly flat.

"My son, do you not recognize me? I ask again, how many humans have been able to invoke me?"

Obviously this was *not* Samael. There was simply too much love in his voice. He didn't know how to respond to the question. He exhaled and flatly said, "Including me... or not?"

The face in the energy grinned.

"Three," he said.

"Their names were Jesus Christ, Mary Magdalene, and now... you."

Calvin felt weak in the knees.

"Who... who... are you?" he stammered.

"It's time you start learning some things. Who am I? I AM... I am ancient, I am the dark... though I am also known as the bearer of light."

Calvin immediately thought of the burning bush story and of God's response when Moses asked his name.

I AM.

In his heart, Calvin knew with whom he was speaking. The enormity of it was overwhelming and he felt like there was a trap door under his heart that suddenly opened. At the same time he didn't want to believe it. All of his previous beliefs about a supreme ruler, or the complete lack of one, were being challenged. He didn't WANT to believe this. Even now, he was too damn stubborn to admit that he could have been wrong.

His mind spun, wondering why someone like him would be chosen by... he didn't even want to say it... God? How did he possibly get in the position to deal with God directly, AND the spirit some say is Satan? It was too much to comprehend. Religious psychos and crackpot freaks talked to God... not Calvin Janek, advertising exec and atheist extraordinaire.

"And my consort, be careful of her," He continued, "She's not evil, but she's as dark as they come; and yet harbors the most beautiful light."

His consort? There are TWO of them? She? At this point Calvin's mind stopped trying to rationalize and he just went with it. Maybe the pagan references to a Goddess were right all along.

"Why should we agree to take Samael's free will, that of our son, away? This is not a small request. Convince each of us of this, and we will bring him to you."

So THAT'S how this was all going to end. It was all up to Calvin now. Elizabeth was out of commission, oblivious to what was happening. And now he had to convince this spirit... this God... to take away Samael's free will, to banish him forever.

Calvin's fantasies of defeating Samael with hexes and spells in a gory fight to the death were replaced by the reality of defeating him with rational thought and love. He thought about what he'd learned so far. About the common theme he heard from all the other spirits.

Love. Trust in love.

He knew what he needed to say.

"Why should you take away his free will? Because his free will is pure evil," he said, "His free will hurts others. His free will kills. His existence is based in revenge-fueled hate and selfish violence. He's not just dark, he's evil. He doesn't know love. He doesn't bring light to this world and we're living in a world in desperate need of light. There's a big difference between dark and evil; Even the darkest of the dark is underlined by true, unconditional love, right? I'm sure your consort has it. Samael does not. No love, no compassion. There's no place for that in this world and that's why I'm going to make sure that this day is his last. I'm done with him. The light always comes after the dark, and it's time for the sun to rise."

His energy began to fade, slowly replaced by the image of a beautiful woman with cascading blonde hair. Her eyes were deep wells that he was sure harbored an untold amount of knowledge about the universe.

"Yes," She said in a seductively feminine voice, "Samael is pure evil now, but we have a long history with him."

She inched closer to him, Her face directly in front of Calvin's.

"Some say I am pure evil too," She whispered into his ear, "What do you think of that?"

"I don't believe it," he said. "If you were pure evil, you wouldn't be here talking with me like this. There's love in you, I can feel it. I can see it in your eyes. You may be dark, but you are *not* evil."

She reached for him and grabbed his thighs. He jumped in surprise that he could feel Her touch. Then it began to hurt, as her long nails pierced his pants and dug into his flesh.

"Oh, the things I could do to you if I were a human again," She said, almost lustfully.

"You are Him, aren't you? I can see my consort in you..."

If she were human, her body would have been pressed up against Calvin's. Her spirit form was sensually close to him, oozing with raw power and pure sexuality. His heart pounded as beads of sweat formed on his forehead. He felt helpless knowing that She could do whatever She wanted to him and he'd be powerless against the pain She could inflict.

She pointed back at Elizabeth, Her eyes still staring into his. She said in a calm yet demanding whisper, "And she is of me. Yes... we have our heirs. The question is, do our heirs have the strength to live their individual truth? To find and know *true* love? To make us proud?"

She slowly ran one hand all the way up his side to his throat, holding it there so Her nails brushed the side of his jugular. He could still feel the pain in his legs and didn't dare move his head out of fear of what She could do to his neck.

"I'm very protective of my heir and I'm not opposed to hurting the men who hurt her. I'm not threatening you, not by any means. After all, you are my son. If you can live your truth, I'll be proud. But I have my doubts."

Her voice was a slow whisper, and She never removed Her eyes from the lock they had on his. She slowly removed Her hand from his neck and he let his head hang.

"Lift your head!" She demanded loudly, "No heir of mine will *ever* hang his head. Grow a spine and hold your head high. Always."

She faded away and was replaced by the bright field of light that was Him.

Calvin's heart still pounded out of his chest and his head spun between past conversations and the knowledge he just gained. The things Seamus had said finally made sense. 'You'll finally come to realize who ye are.'

He didn't have much time to ponder this though, as Samael appeared to the upper right of Him. Samael had what looked like a rope wrapped around his body, his arms tied behind his back. His head hung so his horns pointed directly at him.

"He is bound," the booming voice said.

"But to keep him bound permanently, I believe you know what you need to do..."

The necklace. Between all the nerves and excitement, he had forgotten to ask Elizabeth if she even remembered to bring it. He called her name.

Nothing. He grabbed her bag and opened it, finding a little white box near the top. The necklace was inside.

"One drop of blood from each of you, from the living heirs of us, and this evil will permanently be bound. Do this only if that is what you want."

He didn't need to give it a second thought. His legs were still oozing from where She had grabbed him, so getting his blood was easy. He reached down to his thigh and ran a finger across the small drip of blood he could feel toward his knee, then smeared it into the open necklace.

He didn't have a way to get blood from Elizabeth though, at least not without some pain. He searched her purse looking for something with which he could cut her. He found nothing. Quickly scanning his desk, he saw a pair of scissors and picked them up. Elizabeth was still slumped forward, and he grabbed her hand. He turned her palm face up and extended her pointer finger, quickly slashing it with the open scissors, careful to not go too deep. He let her bleed into the open necklace before applying pressure to her cut by squeezing her finger with his hand.

He clasped the necklace closed, and held it up. The image of Samael, bound forever, faded away.

"It is done," He said, "Tonight, bury that necklace someplace it will never be disturbed."

He nodded.

"Will I hear from you again?"

He had so many questions, but right now just wanted to tell Elizabeth everything.

"You will, my son, your path in the light is just beginning."

Elizabeth began to stir as he faded away and the office slowly returned to its normal state. The candles slowly flickered. One of them had melted into a large pile of wax near the entrance of his office. He briefly wondered how he'd explain that to his coworkers.

He sat next to Elizabeth as she woke, stroking her hair. She looked at him, obviously full of questions.

"It is done," Calvin said, finding His words only fitting.

Elizabeth quietly giggled as she slowly woke up. Then she laughed.

"It's done? He's gone?"

Though laughing, tears streamed down her face.

"Twenty-eight years of dealing with this and it's done? He's gone?"

Calvin nodded.

"Thank you, oh my God, thank you Calvin..." she turned her head so her eyes looked directly into his and placed her hands on his cheeks.

"I love you. I've been feeling it for a long time... I love you."

He wasn't sure how to respond. His mind was a swirling vortex of mush at this point and he was overcome with relief, humbleness, and comfort from Elizabeth all at once.

Maybe she was his true love... maybe the feelings that had developed were true and he was meant to be with this amazing, beautiful woman with whom he shared so much in common.

"I love you, too."

He kissed her, then held her tighter as she cried.

...

On the drive home, Calvin checked his cell phone and found five missed calls from Lisa. Her voicemails started out calmly asking if he was okay, but by the last one she was frantic. He told Elizabeth that Lisa was totally freaked out, and the rest of the drive was silent.

They pulled up to the house and saw his mom's blue Honda SUV in front. They hugged awkwardly, he got out of the car, and Elizabeth pulled out of the driveway to head home. It was an awkward end to an amazingly powerful afternoon.

Calvin entered the house and found Lisa huddled in a quivering heap on the couch. His mom was in Hannah's room with the kids.

Lisa perked up a little when she saw him.

"Oh thank God you're here," she said, "I've been trying to call you! Why didn't you answer!?"

"Lisa I couldn't get to my phone, you wouldn't believe the things I saw today... but relax, it's all done."

He flopped with a large, exhausted exhale onto the couch next to his wife.

Lisa began crying again, and between sobs told him about a panic attack she had in the bathroom just a couple hours earlier.

"Everything was going fine... I had just gotten the kids in the bathtub and was trying not to obsess over what you might be doing and if you were okay. You not answering your phone didn't help.

That's when I could start to feel the panic building inside. I tried to keep it in check and focus on the two beautiful children in front of me. I just couldn't hold on any longer.

I burst into sobs and fell to my knees. The pressure was too much. How could I keep myself composed knowing there was some kind of scary spirit in my son's room and my husband was out fighting an evil spirit with a woman I think he's having an affair with? I sobbed until I couldn't breathe. My stomach contracted and the little amount of air I could get was being forced out by the dry heaves. I hung over the toilet and threw up. I desperately needed to get air but another contraction kept me from breathing. I felt like I was dying, Cal.

Sterling and Hannah watched it all from the bathtub. I can only imagine how scared and helpless they felt. I collapsed and blacked out."

"When I came to," she continued, "I was so scared... and the poor kids...that's when I called your mom to come over," she said, "I just couldn't do it alone anymore."

Calvin remembered something he'd heard from Ellis... 'Samael will try to get to the ones you love if he can't get directly to you.'

"Oh my God Lisa," Calvin said, "I'm so sorry. That explains so much. He wouldn't come to me at first. The coward came to you instead..."

...

Later that night Calvin went out in the backyard to finish the last task required. While alone, he checked his voicemail. A message from Elizabeth waited.

"I'm not sure if you'll check this tonight. I know your love and energy belongs at home right now. I understand that Calvin.

"I've changed today. I'm free. You are free. I know we have more to talk about, especially our life path. Are you going to walk away? I'm left so confused. I feel like you know me so well, even without knowing me fully yet. Tonight my spirit will wander in search of answers. Having to walk away from you after everything today was the hardest thing I've done this week. The ride back to your house was agony. I felt like I went from on top of the world to 10,000 leagues below sea. I felt like a child, lost and born new to the world without direction. Though I feel strong, though I feel free... I won't lie in saying that I also have this gnawing fear that you're giving up. That you just can't, or won't do this anymore. Or that you can't love me.

Please know that I meant it. I love you. No matter what. But if it's just not in you to walk that path, I understand.

My one wish tonight is that you and Lisa are well, cared for, safe, happy, and blessed. I love you both dearly and want you to be whole."

After listening to the message, Calvin, in his soggy and cold backyard, dug a deep hole behind a large evergreen bush, intent on burying the treasured ancient necklace forever.

Chapter 18
Aftershock
Friday, January 27, 2006

Normalcy had yet to return with the 14th nearly two weeks behind them. Samael seemed more like just another step in Calvin's spiritual evolution, albeit a very large one.

Rather than feeling energized and relieved, Calvin felt more tired, worn out, and exhausted then ever. Even making the trip up the short two flights of stairs to his office was fatiguing.

He still enjoyed time with Elizabeth and they routinely found reasons to meet during lunch or after a shoot for drinks, often without the knowledge or consent of either spouse.

The knowledge of who they were provided ample conversation, and enough reason to continue the relationship after the 14th. Calvin wondered if there was more they were supposed to do together. He reasoned that they couldn't stop all contact just because a certain date on the calendar had passed.

The realization of the connection they shared was surreal, yet amplified with every meeting. Over the last two weeks, each time they'd gotten together, one of the two most powerful spirits in the universe, one of Them, would come through and share knowledge or life advice.

It was usually Her. She never once told Elizabeth or Calvin what to do; Just reinforced the idea that whatever happens is by choice. Calvin was learning the power of making life choices, and realizing the consequences of those choices.

Calvin had a hard time wrapping his head around the fact that, just a little more than two months ago, he didn't even know Elizabeth. The elaborate web of events that unfolded during that short amount of time warped his rational mind. As he looked back on them, he knew it wasn't all just 'fate.' Each event was preceded by a choice; starting with the very beginning when he chose to start an uncomfortable conversation with an intriguing blonde who showed up on his set the night before Thanksgiving break. He also felt another choice welling inside him, one that he couldn't ignore. Was Lisa his true love? While the real demon, Samael, was gone, he felt like this decision was an even bigger demon, with severe consequences for whatever choice he made.

These were the thoughts that kept him from giving 100 percent to his work, which was even harder to care about now that he knew the truth about his origins.

Calvin, lost in these thoughts, was rudely interrupted when one of his employees, Helen, a woman in her early 20s, burst into his office.

"I can't take her anymore, Calvin. I won't put up with her talking to me like that."

Calving figured she was talking about Kristy, one of the account executives, and wasn't looking forward to trying to talk Helen down by telling her that her job relied on making sure that people like Kristy got what they needed.

He leaned back in his office chair, grinning to himself as he noticed the candle wax still melted on the carpet at Helen's feet. She sat on the couch facing his desk, her right foot directly next to the wax.

He listened to Helen with one ear, but noticed an email come through and redirected his attention to his screen. It was blank, with a simple period in the subject line. He read it as he pretended to listen to Helen's rant.

I am inclined to speak with you. How foreign it is to wait on anyone. I will allow her to do her bidding and when she is done we shall have words. Until then I will watch you. Allow yourself to feel me.

The presence of Her was nearly overwhelming and he had to wonder if Helen could feel the energy shift. He tried to compose himself and listen to his employee. He just wanted her to leave so he could close himself in his office again.

"You okay?" Helen asked after finishing her rant. "What's with you lately?"

"I've just been under a lot of pressure from Mable and Casey, that's all," he lied, "They've got me working on a lot of things, and I'm a little stressed. No big deal. I'll talk to Kristy for you, okay?"

She seemed satisfied and stood up to leave.

"Hey Helen?" he said as she was leaving.

"Yeah," she said, turning back to him with a smile, probably thinking he was going to open up to her more.

"Close that door on your way out, would you?"

Helen did and he anxiously looked around the room for his visitor.

"I'm ready now," he said.

She appeared not far from where Helen had sat.

"You are quite breathtaking, the way your eyes dart. I am fond of our daily greetings. Even if you don't know I'm here.

"Deal with items as you need to, I am patient when the need comes. Do not feel any less for making me wait."

"I won't make you wait anymore," he said, "You are important."

"Yes I am," She responded, "However, so is life and existing."

"What inquisitive creatures they are, typical women," She continued, apparently referencing Helen's visit.

"That's for sure," he said, "Beautiful creatures though."

"I find them trivial at best," She said, "They are so afflicted in this time and age, so weighted down by issues. Women these days do not seem to be able to face beautiful tragedy with a smile. So many of them have stopped being goddesses."

"I'd like to remember a time when they were," Calvin said.

She grinned and moved closer to him, Her face now directly in front of his.

"When you return home to me, I will show you the paths you've walked, and you will remember. You'll remember the beauty of a sword in a woman's hand, so powerful, so confident, not even your Seamus would challenge her. I'll show you the beauty, truth, and liberating celebrations of Beltane and Samhain. You will remember when women were strong."

He had the image in his head of a beautiful female warrior and asked, "Why must humans forget so easily?"

She backed away from him again, saying, "Forgetfulness is a protection against mockery. There are those destined to walk the elder's path, and those destined to observe. To forget."

As She finished talking, Her eyes squinted as though She was in thought about something.

"I feel your body is weakened, kindred son?"

He paused, interested that She picked up on his exhaustion.

"I've been feeling weak lately. It's hard to even walk up the stairs. I just feel like my muscles have to work a lot harder."

"It's the shift in energy you created when Samael was bound. Anyone who's attuned enough will feel it. You were directly involved, so you will be directly affected. It will pass."

He sat again silent, pondering.

"Today I wait for you to speak," She said, "I observe. Speak in your own time."

Still, he sat silent, finding himself full of questions but not knowing where to start, or what he was even allowed to ask.

"Why do you hesitate to ask me things?" She asked.

"There's so much to ask, so much I want to know, about the world, about Him, about you. I don't know what is okay to ask you and what isn't," he finally said.

"If it is not acceptable you will not get an answer," She said quickly.

Obviously She wanted him to carry this conversation, so he went directly to what he knew best.

"Can you tell him about my children? Their spirits? I want to know anything I can about them, to help them."

"I can and will. Your Sterling is bright. He is everything Elizabeth has said, a healer, an intuit, an empath, a channeler, a diviner, and if he chooses to cling to the path, a practitioner."

"Hannah," She continued, "Is a feeler, an empath. She's a dream visionary and a nurturer."

"Are they old spirits?" he asked.

"Guess which one is," She said with a smile and a slight nod.

"Sterling."

"You are wise," She said proudly.

"I'll always nurture and support them, help guide them," Calvin said.

"You will. But it is not for you to guide their paths, they must find their own path," She said, almost as if it was a reminder to him.

"The hardest thing for ANY parent is to step back and allow his or her heirs to live their existence," She continued, obviously referring to both Her 'parenthood' as well as Calvin's.

"It's difficult even for us to allow our heirs the pleasure of what we work for constantly. The pleasure to exist. To experience. I do not want you afraid of anything, ever."

She paused, then looked directly into his eyes and intensely said, "And you've just begun living."

"So let us speak of celebrations and family meetings," She said, apparently changing the subject.

"Yeah..." he replied, "Tomorrow is my son's 4th birthday party."

"What a brilliant and proud day for you!" She said, "Know I will bless him tomorrow," She said.

"Wow, that means a lot. That little guy is so incredibly special to me."

"Both of your children are. All children are," She said, "Perfect little beings."

"They are. Are they the reason I chose to marry Lisa in this life?"

He wanted some kind of clue from Her as to where his true love lay.

"There are many reasons you chose to marry Lisa in this life," She said, not giving him the direction for which he hoped.

Giving up on that topic for now, he wanted to know more about Her.

"Why don't people know about you? Doesn't it bother you that most people shun the idea of a Goddess? Or if they believe in one, they think you're an evil being?"

"People believe what they choose to believe. As long as they are living their truth, I'm not going to judge their human beliefs. They gain full knowledge when they return to the universal energy. As for evil, there is none that comes through when invoking me. The vile creatures know better than to impede on my space and time."

"So you come through for others?" he asked, thinking of the three people who have invoked Him.

"I inspire others. Some music comes from me. I revel in providing muse in an artist's lyrics," She said with a knowing grin, "I believe there's been some you've been partial to lately? You'll always know when an artist has been touched by me. And there will be more. You'll find them, assuming you don't... fall from grace," She said with a wink.

"So that's how I 'come through' for others," She continued, "Though if petitioned correctly, I will aid. But never communicate. Save for my heirs," She said.

"I was thinking that'd be the case."

"You are quite wise," She replied, "You ARE His son after all. Remember to watch for me at the party...Now I take leave."

With that, She faded away, but left a swirling field of energy in Her place.

"I'll watch for you," Calvin said.

"You know not to whom you speak," came the voice, shallow and distant.

He was confused, was this Him? He didn't sound the same as He did on the 14th.

"Whom am I speaking with?"

"Dare you ask and again not know your father?" he replied, taking His now recognizable form. "We shall speak soon, when there is more time. I have known better than to impede on my love's time with you."

"I look forward to our next time," Calvin said, excited and comforted to hear from Him.

"The time draws near where father and son must sit and speak of life and plans, of pride and strength," he said, "Go forth in your day, hold your spine strong and your head high. You are my pride. We will both be near you tomorrow as we are now. Go in peace and love."

"I'll always strive to make you proud," he said in a feeble attempt to reply in an equally eloquent manner.

He left Calvin to tend to the remaining responsibilities of his workday. Before he went back to working though, he called Elizabeth to remind her of Sterling's party tomorrow. She of course remembered and could hardly wait to meet his entire family.

And he was equally excited to introduce her to them.

Chapter 19
Ships in the Night
Monday, January 30, 2006

Calvin arrived at work on Sterling's birthday still high from the weekend's party. Elizabeth got to meet his brothers and parents and they even discovered that she and Calvin's younger brother, James, had lived in the same apartment building at the same time in college.

It was another coincidence that proved hard to wrap his head around and remained at the top of his mind as he began his morning with some online research into Lilith the Goddess.

His search revealed all sorts of conjecture, ranging from speculation on whether or not a female deity exists, to Her role as a murderer of children.

He shook his head and wondered how one day he could get the truth out to the world. She deserved it. Again deciding to avoid work for as long as possible, Calvin logged into his messenger and immediately found a new message.

To the moon...and back says:
The celebration was amazin'
Did ye like our little gift to ye, about James?

Seamus. It had been a while since they last were able to talk.

CALVIN says:
That he lived near Elizabeth on campus?

To the moon...and back says:

Aye
We hid that from her memory, figured it would be a
nice surprise and validation that we've been keepin'
ye close all these years

CALVIN says:
That was amazing.

To the moon...and back says:
In fact brother, when you were there to visit James,
the one time you made it to his campus, do ye recall
commenting on the sorority stuff on one of the
doors?

CALVIN says:
Actually, I do remember that! The entire door was
covered in a collage of pictures- It looked like they
were having so much fun.

To the moon...and back says:
Aye...Welcome to Elizabeth's room, brother. In fact,
the picture she showed ya of Ellis was on that door

Could that be true? The hair on his neck stood on
end. It was such a fleeting moment in time,
seemingly meaningless, but he DID remember
glancing at that door.

To the moon...and back says:

They were both in there that moment too brother. Laughing, drinking their chocolate milk, and lookin' at bridal magazines. They emerged not long after you left.

CALVIN says:
No way... my God... remember goosebumps? I've got 'em

To the moon...and back says:
goose what?

CALVIN says:
Umm... the chills on your skin? The raised bumps on your arms, the back of your neck?

To the moon...and back says:
Aye... the shivers

CALVIN says:
So she's always been close... but just out of sight, just out of reach?

To the moon...and back says:
Aye, you two were like ships passin' in the night

CALVIN says:
Didn't you want so badly for us to run into each other? Though I guess we would have never had a connection at that point...

To the moon...and back says:

It wasn't time yet, but fook yes. Though yer right, there would have been chemistry, but no connection.

To the moon...and back says:
Want to know another memory?

CALVIN says:
Yes!

To the moon...and back says:
The commercial shoot wasn't yer first time physically together

CALVIN says:
Really?! When?

To the moon...and back says:
It was so passing that ye probably don't recall
As ye rode down the elevator from the dorm later that day, she stood in the back corner, her face in some mail...ye wouldn't have seen her face. So you never really "saw" her.
But it was an imprint clue in yer mind and spirit, so when you saw her later in life, you'd FEEL like ye had seen her before. Her scent would breed a sense of familiarity.

Calvin's "shivers" intensified. He was amazed, once again, at how the most minor of details could come together and be so relevant, so much later in life. It was details like this that just couldn't be fabricated, and helped him believe in everything.

CALVIN says:

She was in that elevator? Man, you guys are good.

To the moon...and back says:
No brother, you are good. The lot of ye.

CALVIN says:
There's so much that the lot of YOU do to help us, though.

To the moon...and back says:
Look brother, after this, my words are done for the day. Listen carefully.
If ye can be honest with anyone, be honest with yerself.
This life tis about livin the experience....

It seemed like being honest with oneself would be so easy. Again, this conversation just left him wondering what he wanted out of life. Was a life with Lisa what he intended? Did he want to be with her for the rest of his life? Were there more experiences he wanted? Was he truly happy in his current life, or just entirely too comfortable with the complacency of it?

Chapter 20
The Pain of Honesty
Saturday, February 4, 2006

As Lisa slept in, Calvin called his parents to ask if he could bring the kids over for a few hours. They of course agreed, always happy to have some time with their grandkids.

In the conversation today, he had to be clear that his thoughts and feelings about the marriage were only about him, and not about another woman.

He nervously waited for Lisa to emerge from the bedroom, going over her possible reactions to his words over and over in his head. Would she throw him out? Burst into uncontrollable sobs? He just wasn't sure, and he wasn't looking forward to the look on her face when he told her he wasn't in love with her anymore.

Lisa came out of the bedroom wearing her robe and gave the kids big hugs.

"Good morning," Calvin said somberly, "We're taking the kids to my parents' house this morning. Go ahead and get dressed."

"How come?" she asked.

"I just want us to be alone for a while so we can talk." Lisa slowly nodded, and turned back toward the bedroom to get dressed. He made sure the kids were dressed and ready to head out the door by the time she was finished getting ready.

"So what are you two going to do?" his mom asked as Sterling and Hannah ran into their grandparents' house.

"Just have some time together," he quickly replied. It was one of the most awkward and nerve-wracking moments of his life, knowing what he was about to blindside Lisa with. He was so tempted to just slide it under the carpet and go out and have some fun. Not only would this conversation affect their relationship forever, but the entire dynamic of their extended family and friends.

Their marriage wasn't a bad one. Before these last few months, they rarely fought. They were compatible in going through their day-to-day motions. They agreed on finances as well as on how to raise the children. But a few facts remained: Lisa wasn't his confidant, she belittled him, he didn't feel in love with her, and lately he was feeling like a life with her was not his truth.

Calvin wondered what others would think of his rationalization. People didn't just go around in this world talking about "their truth" in day-to-day conversation. The topic though had become dear to his heart and affected the core of his being. It was something ingrained in the spiritual lessons from the last several months, a term that at first didn't make much sense but now held a huge area of his life's balance. A life, he perceived, which was in a state of incredible imbalance.

Destroying his marriage was not what he wanted to do, but he couldn't help but question the depths of his love to this woman who had been part of his life for so long. Was he really in love with her? Or did he just love her? But how could he say that to someone with whom he had been for a dozen years? They were married, had children, a home, and car loans. Things could get messy.

But he knew that postponing this conversation would only be postponing the inevitable.

Back in the car and rounding the corner away from his parents' house, Lisa spoke up.

"So what's going on, Calvin?" she said as she drove. His heart pounded and his palms began to sweat. He wanted so badly to ignore everything and just carry on with life as usual. The thought of hurting Lisa tore him apart and he couldn't bear seeing hurt on her face. Maybe he could just leave things as they were.

That, he decided, was exactly the problem though. Why should he accept a life for which he felt he had settled? Why live in complacency? He forced the words out of his mouth when he desperately wanted to hold them in.

"I want to talk about us. About our marriage," he said quietly.

"Okay... I'm listening," Lisa replied.

"Okay. Umm, do you ever stop and think about WHY we got married?"

"Because we loved each other and wanted to spend our life together," Lisa quickly replied.

Calvin tried to swallow his words.

"Well, the thing is, I'm not sure that's the case with me. Or at least, remains the case today."

Lisa looked at him, without saying a word.

"I think back to when we got married," he continued, "And a part of me wonders if I only married you because I was afraid I'd hurt your feelings if I didn't." He let the words hang there for a moment, actually quite shocked that he finally said it out loud. It felt like a dream.

"So you're saying you don't love me?" Lisa asked.

"What I'm saying is... I need to figure out if I am IN love with you. I know I love you, but I need to search myself and figure out what I want, Lisa. I'm so sorry to do this to you."

They arrived home and Calvin pulled the Audi into the garage. They both got out without speaking and headed into the house. They sat on the couch at opposite ends and faced each other. Calvin knew this conversation had just begun.

"Can I just explain my thinking for a minute?" he asked, secretly hoping he'd say something that would make sense to her and help her understand.

"I sure wish you would," Lisa said abruptly.

He was amazed at how well she composed herself so far. Her head was held high and she spoke in a strong voice. He had imagined that she would have crumbled by now, and wondered why she hadn't.

"I think back across our entire relationship, and you know what I see? A series of next steps. We started dating, which was great, and pretty soon you were talking about getting married. We were, what, 17, when that topic came up? I was scared about that thought, but liked you a lot and didn't want to hurt you. Or lose you. So I went with it. And then, we're 18 and you started looking at engagement rings. I remember when I proposed that I said that we should take our relationship to the next level. At the time, it seemed like a natural progression. So engaged at 19, we were going to wait until we graduated from college before we got married. Somehow, we started talking about just getting married before we moved for college. You didn't want to live with me before we got married because of what your parents would think. I didn't want to lose you and I didn't want to hurt you. At the time, I still wasn't even sure if I wanted to get married. So when I look back at all this, I just see a relationship filled with next steps. Like we did things because they were just the things that people in relationships did. Soon we had a child, then another, and here we are now. We were married at 20 years old, Lisa. We were just kids. People change over time. Is any of this making sense to you? Haven't you ever thought about this?"

He could see the dreaded hurt on her face now. She was still strong, though obviously sad and angry. His heart broke.

"Are you saying you were never in love with me? I don't believe that. Not for a second. What about all of the fights we had as teenagers? I was ready to give up numerous times. I remember asking you if it would just be easier to break up. I didn't want to deal with the problems in the relationship. It seemed easier to me to walk away. But you wouldn't let that happen. You could have walked away at any time. You had numerous options on many, many occasions, yet you didn't."

She continued, letting her anger fuel her rebuttal. "And I remember quite well you telling ME how ready you were to have kids. It scared the shit out of me. And I wasn't ready."

"You can't imagine how hard it is for me to look at you and tell you these things Lisa. I'm not saying I was never in love with you. I'm questioning whether or not I am now."

"No, that's not what you said a couple of minutes ago Calvin. You made it sound as though you felt coerced into dating and marrying me. It's insulting. This slighted view of your past... it doesn't even seem like we have the same memories. You have been so messed up lately Calvin. Like you are under a goddamn spell. And I am getting sick of it. The words I hear you saying don't even sound like they are coming from you. It sounds like you are regurgitating some spiritual shit that you think you are supposed to be saying."

"Obviously, this is about Elizabeth," she continued, "Are you having an affair? Are you just trying to say these things so I get pissed and kick you out so you can go live your life with her? Are you so weak that you can't leave me, so you need to force the issue with me so I am the one who makes the move? Well I am not going to allow you to force me to be the reason our marriage ends, so that when the kids are older you can tell them that I am the one who kicked your sorry little ass out!"

Lisa's anger was obviously rising and her demeaning words, though amplified now, were part of the reason for the conversation in the first place. Calvin was still surprised that she was taking the angry vs. emotionally devastated route.

"No Lisa," he said with a sigh, "I'm not having an affair with Elizabeth."

He knew he was falling for Elizabeth, but figured that wouldn't have happened had his marriage been strong in the first place.

"I don't know what the future holds with her. Maybe I am supposed to be with her. Maybe not. I'll admit that meeting her and the contact with the spirits has given me the strength to say these things, because I need to live my truth. And I'm not sure if this current life is my truth, or if I've just become complacent in settling for it."

Lisa interrupted.

"Calvin, that doesn't even sound like you!"

"Well that's part of the problem. I don't even think that you know who I am. You know who I was, and this is who I am now. So what we need to do is decide that if you and I met right now, would you want to date me? Would I ask you to marry me? I think, if I decide that's a yes, I'll ask you to marry me again and hope you say yes. We'll even get new rings."

Lisa's cheeks flushed in anger again. Her eyes welled with tears, but none rolled down her cheeks. Calvin cried first, feeling the lump in his throat burst and feeling the tears pour.

"This is the hardest thing I've ever done Lisa," he choked out, looking at her through his tear-blurred vision.

"I don't even know how to respond to this right now," she said, "So I'm just supposed to carry on with life as normal, while you take whatever time you need to figure out if you want to stay married to me? Or what, remarry me? What does that say about me? Who do you think I am? That I am so weak, so dependent on you that my entire world will fall apart without you? That I am going to let you treat me like shit, and sit here pining after you while you reinvent yourself? Everybody changes. Do you think that people who get married at 30 are the same people at 45? Hell no. You are not the only one who is a different person at 28 than he was at 15. You are so full of yourself. Just exactly how much time do you envision me waiting around to see if my husband will propose to me again, after he's figured out if I am good enough to stay married to, or if he wants to dump everything for some hot new blonde?"

"I think we'll both just know, Lisa. I can't just say I'll know in two weeks. I can't put a time limit on this. I guess we just go day by day and see how things go," he said.

Lisa, although angry, but still amazingly composed said, "I'm convinced that this is all about Elizabeth, like you're just trying to bide your time with me until it's convenient for you to leave and go to her."

"Lisa, I told you, this is about you and me. About me figuring out who I am, who I want to be. I'm not sure if this current life is what I want, and I need to figure it out."

This time he verbalized his thoughts.

"And if our marriage was strong, in the first place, Elizabeth wouldn't even be an issue right now. I'm not biding my time with you for her. I just need to figure myself out first."

"I don't believe it. I can't look at you anymore, I can't talk about this anymore. I'm going to take a bath," she said.

As she walked down the hallway, she turned to say one last thing, "You can stay here and try to figure yourself out, but there are no guarantees on how long I'm going to put up with being treated like shit. Don't assume I'll always be around waiting for you. If you want this to work, you need to really work at this marriage."

Calvin sat on the couch, his face in his hands as he thought about the conversation. It felt good to finally get those words out, and he was surprised that Lisa kept herself composed so well. She never even cried. He wiped the tear stains from his cheeks and left to go pick up the kids. He figured having them around for the rest of the day would be a good diversion from the conversation. He knew there was no going back to normal now; he'd just changed his relationship with Lisa forever.

Chapter 21
Time for a Break
Friday, February 17, 2006

Calvin returned home after writing the letter in his office, and placed the note on the kitchen counter for Lisa to read when she woke up.

She must have gotten up without him hearing because she burst into the bedroom at 8 a.m. holding the letter and speaking at a pace Calvin's still-asleep brain couldn't fully process.

"What is this!? Did you even write this? These don't sound like your words. It doesn't sound like your voice. You need to see a shrink Calvin."

More awake now, Calvin sat up in bed.

"Look... Lisa, my intent with that letter was to comfort you and try to help you see my point, to understand my side."

"It didn't work, Cal. This is psychobabble. You do not speak or write like this. You're not being yourself!"

"That's the problem. The Calvin who wrote that note is the guy you're married to. You should try to get to know him."

"You're having a mid-life crisis. No. You're having a quarter-life crisis. You're questioning to the core of yourself and what you're doing with your life, while questioning what you imagine yourself doing 10 years from now. That's textbook, Calvin. I think you'll get over it and come to your senses, but I need some time away. I can't do this."

"So what's your plan?" Calvin asked.

"I called my mom, we are taking the kids out of town for the weekend. I packed their stuff, I'm picking my mom up in 15 minutes, and we'll be back Sunday or Monday. Maybe. I hope you reflect this weekend and figure stuff out, Calvin."

Lisa turned and left. He could hear her gather the kids and felt the walls of the house shake as she closed the door to the garage behind them.

He was alone.

He smiled, and got out of bed.

Calvin discovered that, before Lisa left, she had put all of her scrap-booked picture albums and home video DVDs on the coffee table. Apparently she wanted him to reflect on their marriage, their life, and their kids, hoping they'd have an influence and snap him back into reality.

Next to the albums was a note.

Dear Calvin,
It is clear to me that we could both benefit from some time apart, to think about our marriage and the path that we want to take from here.
I hope that while we are gone, you will really think about what you are doing, and the long-term ramifications that the decision now will have on not only your future, but that of our children.
Maybe we should consider marriage counseling. Think about it, and we'll talk when I come home.
Lisa

"Hmm," he said aloud, "A free weekend... Cool."

He put away the scrapbooks and DVDs, knowing that he had no intention of reminiscing about the past.

He called Elizabeth right away and asked her to meet for drinks after work. He was excited for no curfew and no questions when he got home.

...

On the way to the bar, Calvin felt some guilt and called Lisa's cell phone. She answered.
"Hey Lisa, be safe this weekend, okay?"
"We will. Don't worry," she replied curtly.
"And yes, I'll think about counseling. It might be good,"
"Thanks Calvin, I hope you think this weekend. We'll be back Sunday night. Bye," she said, and hung up.
He was surprised she was so short on the phone, but his guilt went away and he grinned as he pushed on the accelerator and sped toward Elizabeth.

Chapter 22
Alone
Sunday, February 19, 2006

Calvin enjoyed the hell out of his weekend alone. His Friday night out drinking with Elizabeth and her friends was a karaoke-fest. Being seen in public with Elizabeth, as a couple, invigorated him. They held hands, laughed, hugged, and even shared a soul-igniting kiss before the evening ended.

He wondered if that night was the one that pushed him across the line of having an affair.

Most of Saturday was spent in recovery mode, lying in bed, and reading while trying to distract his mind from the possibilities Elizabeth held.

Saturday night he was invited to a night of poker with some coworkers, which he accepted.

He awoke early Sunday morning wanting to do something a little different. He knew he had time to do whatever he wanted, and the possibilities seemed endless. Elizabeth was home with Jack for the weekend, so whatever he decided on had to be as a party of one.

He settled on taking himself on a long drive: Seattle. Seattle had always been something of a haven for him, always able to make him feel relaxed; even among the miles of traffic jams and clogged streets. He loved being near water and today he craved it.

With no one to answer to, he headed for the freeway. By 10 a.m., he entered the heart of the Emerald City. The sun shone brilliantly, glistening off the water of Puget Sound. Mount Rainer stood majestically in the distance, and the snow-capped peaks of the Cascades and the Olympic Mountains surrounded him. He felt at home, and at peace. There was no other city in the world as beautiful as Seattle on a sunny day.

Driving straight for the waterfront, he found a space to park on the street and wandered up and down the wharf. The smell of the salt water and fresh breeze energized his spirit.

With his mind clear, he took deep satisfying breaths, filling his lungs with the crisp, fresh February air. He could feel Them around him, and felt reassured that he was on the right path, though he knew some very challenging obstacles lay in front of him.

But for now, this is exactly what he needed; to get away, to get near the water and just... feel. Just... be. Though the waterfront was packed with families, tourists, and the occasional jogger, he felt fantastically alone. He leaned against the railing outside a bustling seafood restaurant and silently looked over Puget Sound, taking in the scents of the fresh ocean water.

He also caught a hint of the smell of fried food, and thinking about food for the first time since arriving in the city, he left the waterfront and walked up the Pike Street hill in search of lunch.

He found an Irish restaurant that he'd never seen before, and thinking of Seamus, entered. Inside was a group of about 10 people sitting in a circle, playing traditional Irish music. The sounds of fiddles, flutes, and pennywhistles filled the air. He wondered if this is how the music sounded when Seamus and he lived. It was the perfect backdrop to lunch.

After, he headed north to the University of Washington campus, which he hadn't set foot on since graduation. He wandered the campus, remembering how alone he felt there. Since he was married and living off campus, his college days were simply full of classes, with none of the parties the single life would have provided him. He wondered what his college days would have been like had he not gotten married so early.

Lisa wouldn't have been my one and only, that's for sure. The smooth red bricks on the ground of Red Square gave way to the old majestic brick buildings that towered above him. The campus was virtually empty from his perspective, except for one other person on the opposite side of the square. He walked toward her, asking if she'd take his picture. Removing the camera from his pocket, he handed it to her and stepped back. She snapped the image. He thanked her, took his camera back and headed for his car feeling refreshed and at peace.

With a long drive still ahead of him, he headed for home. He arrived at 7 p.m with the garage still empty, signaling that he beat his family home. Excited to see his kids, but nervous to see his wife, he wondered how he'd tell her about his carefree weekend.

As he waited for them to return, he logged onto the computer to download the picture from Red Square. Looking closely, he noticed a large smear over his right shoulder. On such a bright, clear sunny day, there's only one thing that could be. Perhaps he wasn't alone on campus after all.

The sound of the garage door opening made Calvin's heart jump. He glanced out the window and could see Lisa's Honda turning the corner. A quick glance at his watch told him that it was just after 8. Lisa must have already fed the kids dinner before coming home.

He shut down the computer and waited by the laundry room for his family to enter the house.

"Hi Daddy," little Hannah drawled as she toddled in the door behind Sterling, who barely looked up at him and didn't say a word.

"Hi my little sweetheart," Calvin said and gave her a hug.

"Hey Lisa, what's the matter with Sterling?" he said as she came in with an armful of bags and a plastic bag.

"Hey," she tiredly replied, "Sterling is sick. He puked at Mom and Dad's, inside a tent. He hasn't been able to hold anything down all day; he's running a temperature and I'm afraid he's dehydrated. Neither of us got any sleep last night; it's been a rough 24 hours. But that's what being a parent is all about. Being there in the good and bad times."

"Nice jab," Calvin retorted, not wanting to let her snide remark go unnoticed.

She wiped a piece of hair out of her eyes as she set the bags and large garbage sack down.

"How was your weekend by yourself? Did you have some time to look at the albums?"

He felt a little guilty for what he was about to say, but it was the truth.

"No, I didn't look at them. I had a fantastic weekend, actually."

Lisa shoved the plastic bag that held Sterling's puke-filled clothes out of the way and made her way into the living room. She was obviously formulating her response, but her face couldn't hide the disappointment.

"Well I'm glad you enjoyed your little vacation," she said sharply as she emptied the bags and started a load of laundry.

She turned her attention to Sterling, who was sitting listlessly on the couch, watching them.

"Honey, do you want to go and get your pajamas on? You probably should just take it easy on the couch for a while. How about I'll give you a special popsicle after you get your jammies on, okay sweetie?"

She walked over and gave his hot little forehead a kiss.

"Okay Mommy...." said Sterling, his reply tired and soft.

Lisa walked with him into his bedroom and picked a pair of pajamas out of his top dresser drawer.

"Here baby. You put these on while I go wash your sleeping bag. When you are done, come out into the living room and I'll get you that popsicle."

She gave him a little hug and headed out the door. Hannah had followed her into Sterling's bedroom, rubbing her eyes and looking completely worn out. Obviously Hannah hadn't slept well either. And now that she had been exposed to the flu, she needed to get to bed right away.

Lisa took Hannah into her room, put her to bed, and returned to the kitchen to finish the conversation.
"So what'd you do with all your time then? Maybe I'm the one who should have left by myself, so you were in the trenches with the kids."
Lisa walked into the laundry room, followed by Calvin, and pulled the tent out of the garbage sack and stuffed it into the washer.
"Well, I went and played poker with some coworkers, and today I drove to Seattle and back," he said nonchalantly. He left out the enchanting night with Elizabeth.
"Seattle!? Why?" she asked, "Oh wait, I know. You took Elizabeth with you, didn't you? Christ, Calvin, if you added a physical aspect to this emotional affair... This marriage is over."
"First of all," he said, "I went alone. I felt like I needed to be there to think. I just figured that breathing the fresh air and being closer to the water was what I needed. It felt really good and gave me time by myself."
"So what conclusions did you come to with so many hours of solitude?" she asked.
"I didn't make any real decisions, just had some time for myself to start sorting things out," he said.
"You're incredible. You seriously think I'm just going to sit around and wait for you to decide if you want me, don't you? What kind-of person do you think I am? You think his entire world revolves around you?"

Before waiting for his reply, she added, "Do I need to start looking for houses? You know that if we get a divorce I won't be able to afford to stay here and still work part time. And just because you don't want to be married to me anymore, doesn't mean that I want to work all of the time just to make ends meet. I will not be cheated out of time with my children."

Sterling, who had finished putting on his pajamas and walked into the living room without Lisa or Calvin noticing, said, "Mommy, I don't want a new house, I like my blue bedroom."

He sounded scared, and his voice was so small. Calvin felt tears welling in his eyes.

Lisa came out of the laundry room and walked over to him. She wanted to be honest and not lie to him about what was going on.

"Well Sterling," Lisa said, crouching down to his level so that she could make eye contact, "If Daddy decides he doesn't want to live with us anymore, we are going to have to move."

Lisa looked at him, hoping that this conversation was having some effect on him.

"Lisa, if this doesn't work between us, I'll make sure you don't have to move. I'll pay the house payment; I want our kids to keep the stability of this house. Please don't use the kids as leverage, it's not fair to them."

Those words seriously hurt his heart; he didn't want to think of his kids having to move.

"Oh really? You obviously aren't thinking clearly. How could we take the same amount of money that we make now, and be able to pay to run a separate household for you too? Besides, I wouldn't want your help, or your charity. My parents raised me not to be dependent on anyone. I am a self-sufficient, independent woman with a good stable job. I would make things work without your help."

She scooped up Sterling and kissed him on his soft hair.

"No, we'd move. The kids would adapt and be fine," she said.

She set Sterling down on the couch and went over to the freezer to pull out a popsicle. Opening the wrapper, she walked over and handed it to him. His eyes looked almost sunken, and he was pale except for the flush of fever on his cheeks.

"Well, hopefully we don't have to worry about that yet. After I talked with you on Friday, a counselor that I had left a message with called me back. We have an appointment for next Monday. She seems really neat, Calvin. I think that she can help us a lot. Thanks for agreeing to try it."

He didn't know what to say. He really didn't want to go to counseling. And he knew that he needed to be honest with Lisa about that.

"Lisa, I might have changed my mind about that. I don't know if I want to go to counseling."

Lisa didn't even have time to react to what he had just told her. Just as she opened her mouth to reply, a loud cracking sound came from the laundry room, followed by the sound of the washing machine grinding to a halt. They looked at each other as they both registered what they heard next as the sound of gushing water.

They ran across the living room and stopped at the doorway to the laundry room. A river of water flowed out of the bottom of the machine and across the floor, already crossing the doorway and onto the wood floors in the dining area.

"Oh my God, go grab some towels!" Lisa yelled as she wiped away tears.

Calvin was secretly delighted at the timing of the break, which surely halted a fierce fight.

He returned with virtually every towel they owned and began soaking up the water. The washer had apparently been full when it broke, creating a cascading waterfall; a super capacity sized tub of water all over the floor. It was a major mess.

"It's still under warranty, I'll get someone out here tomorrow to fix it," Calvin said.

Lisa took the clothes out of the washer and stuffed them in garbage bags that she had grabbed from under the kitchen sink while Calvin grabbed the towels.

It took a while to mop up the mess. By the time they were finished, they had dirtied every one of the large bath towels they owned.

"I need to go to my mom and dad's to wash these so we have clean towels after we shower tomorrow. I'll be back in a while."

She walked over to Sterling and gave him a kiss.

"Honey, I need to go to Grandpa and Grandma's for a little while to wash all of these towels, okay? You can just lie here and finish your popsicle. After you're done, I want you to go to bed so that you can work on getting better, okay honey?"

"Okay Mommy. I will. I love you," he replied quietly. She hugged him and walked back to the laundry room. Lisa grabbed the bags, opened the door and carried them into the garage without another word to him.

Calvin slowly closed the door behind her and walked over to unplug the dryer. He didn't need a 220-volt appliance sitting in a puddle of water.

He was torn inside, but felt like he was making the right choice and being true to himself. It killed him to see Lisa so hurt, but he saw his thinking as completely rational and felt proud of telling Lisa he didn't want to go with her. Yes, he convinced himself he was making the right choice.

With the water leak under control, he went to talk to Sterling.

"Sterling, I love you kiddo."

"I love you too, Daddy," he said.

"Whatever happens, I will always love you. Forever. You'll always be my little guy. I'll always be your daddy."

"I know, Daddy," he said.

Sterling was stoic, munching on his popsicle, and Calvin wondered how much of the talk he registered. Figuring he wasn't getting through to him, he thought he'd just show his love through his actions. He put his arm around his little guy and held him tight. He just needed to be by his son at that moment.

...

After putting Sterling to bed, Calvin went down to the basement to change a long-overdue furnace filter. He heard footsteps coming down the stairs and prepared for Lisa's onslaught. Instead, Lisa's eyes welled with tears at the simple sight of her husband performing this simple maintenance chore. She cried.

"I don't know how I'd do this by myself," she sobbed. "What do I have to do Calvin?" she continued. "Do I need to get on my knees and beg you to try counseling? To give us a shot?"

She lowered herself to her knees and wrapped her arms around his ankles, her face buried at his feet. He looked down on her, the image of his wife literally begging at his feet made him realize just how badly he was hurting her.

She looked up at him and said, "Because I'll get down here and beg you. Please. PLEASE, don't give up on me, on us, on our kids..." Lisa said as the crying continued.

As he looked down on her, he felt the familiar lump in his throat grow. Maybe he was wrong. Maybe he did have a great situation here at home. Here was his wife, begging for a second chance. How could he say no to her?

"Stand up, Lisa, please. Stand up," he said tearfully. She slowly rose and looked into his eyes.

"Okay...okay," he said as he pulled her into him and held her tight.

Chapter 23
The Big Bang
Monday, February 20, 2006

Calvin wanted to spend as little time at home as possible and left home before Lisa woke up. He was frustrated that, in a weak moment, he had promised his wife that he would go to counseling next week. At least he still had a week to figure out how to get out of it.

While getting situated at work, a familiar feeling settled over his office. In the corner, to the right of and slightly above his couch, formed the image of Him.

"It's time I begin telling you my story. At least, the beginning of it," He said, "I see you struggling in your decisions, and while we'll never pressure you one way or the other, hearing some of my story may provide inspiration for you."

"Wow, okay," Calvin replied, stunned at His sudden presence, "I'd love to hear your story."

"Any knowledge you wish, I will tell you. And those are powerful words for me to tell to a mortal human," He said.

"What's your name?" The question suddenly erupted from Calvin's mouth.

"My name... my true name has been clouded by time and corrupted by lies. For now, my name is I AM. In time, you'll be privy to the truth. What other questions do you have?"

"We have time in the future for me to ask questions of you," Calvin said, "What did you want to tell me today?"

"As I said, you should know the beginning of my story. In the beginning," He said, "And by that I mean the beginning of EVERYTHING, there were two energies. Just... two. No planets, no galaxies, no biological life. This is before the universe and time as you know it."

Calvin was already enthralled. Was he about to hear how the universe came into being? Could the most debated question in all of science be answered, right here in his humble little office?

He continued, "I was one of those energies, She being the other. We searched for each other, existing independently in silence... before time, before biology, before gravity, before everything. I knew there was another, I knew She existed, but I had to wait... in the void of nothingness, until our paths crossed. When they finally did, our energies collided, our spirits fused... in a big... bang."

The words hung in the air for a moment before Calvin could put them together.

"The Big Bang?" he repeated, his heart pounding inside his chest, his breathing fast and shallow. "YOU were the Big Bang?"

Had he been standing, he would have stumbled at hearing these words.

"Yes. And thus, the universe was started," He said, "The biology of evolution began. And with biology, we were able to create more spirits in our own image. We waited, and we watched the beauty of life evolve from that single moment."

The eternal debate of evolution versus creation was just made incredibly clear; and only to Calvin. He was mesmerized by the significance of what he heard, even though it seemed to make perfect sense. Why hadn't he ever heard a theory about biology being created, and then evolving and taking its course? Why had the mythology of current religion taken such a hold on the modern world? How could man be arrogant enough to say that God created humans in his own image, when the human image didn't even exist when the 'biology of evolution' began?

"When the time came that our spirits could take human form on Earth," He continued, "We did. But just once. We've always taken pride in watching spirits experience being human. We watch them learn what it means to exist, to experience, and to truly live. We watch what choices they make, and see them either suffer or be rewarded by the consequences of their choices. We always watch with unconditional love for them all, even when they fall from grace."

"You lived once?" Calvin asked, surprised to hear that He had lived as a man. Calvin wondered at the power He must have had as a human.

"Yes, though even I fell from grace," He said, "Though my consort may tell you otherwise."

"How?" he asked, "How does someone fall from grace?"

"That's a question for you to figure out, and it's different for each human. I'll tell you my story, in time," He said.

He continued, "My consort and I experienced being human together, and we fell in love even as humans. But another man was trying to win her heart... Can you guess who that was?"

Calvin didn't even know where to begin, and just shook his head.

"You knew him as Samael. Samael lived many human lives and, at one time, he was honorable. He was strong, loving, sensual, happy... and potent. As a human, the attention of people around him, especially women, was something he began to take for granted. It became an expectation, not a flattery. His energy didn't just attract attention, but demanded it. Samael ate it all up, directing his time and energy toward building his notoriety and, as long as he had a harem of women, wasn't concerned with love or anything deeper than superficial status symbols. And that, my son, is what began eating away at Samael. His once radiant eyes slowly lost their gentle, caring look. They cooled to a distant glimmer; an aggressive darkness that harbored ambition not yet obtained. His spirit was slowly dying. On his last journey to the human side of the veil, Samael's arrogance had grown so strong that he felt receiving attention was his given right, whether earned or not. His last human experience was during my only human experience, and he wanted my consort. Despite all of his advances, she turned him down and remained focused only on me. Our love was true love. Samael couldn't understand why my consort didn't want him. So he killed her. He took her from me in life. The consequences of his choices have spanned the ages. So I tell you: Don't fall from grace."

Those proved to be his last words, as he disappeared and left Calvin alone in his office, bewildered at the knowledge he just gained and again questioning what he was meant to do with it all.

Don't fall from grace.

Was it a warning to not stray from the path of truth he'd been on? Would going to the appointment next Monday be a fall from grace, because he'd only be going to make Lisa happy?

That had to be it.

The morning flew by, with seemingly insignificant work fires in to put out. As his stomach grumbled in hunger, he realized that he had forgotten his lunch in his haste to leave the house that morning.

His phone rang as he pulled into a drive-thru of a fast food restaurant.

'Lisa calling' was displayed on the Caller ID. Instead of proceeding through the drive thru, he pulled his car into the back of the lot, just underneath an overpass of I-90.

"Hi Lisa," he answered.

"Hey, I was just calling to tell you what the washing machine guy had to say," she said.

He realized that he had forgotten to call this morning like he had promised. Lisa must have called and apparently they sent someone right away. He was relieved to have a somewhat normal conversation with her for a change.

"Oh yeah. What did he have to say?"

"Well, the entire porcelain tub of the machine is cracked in half. He said that in 20 years of fixing washing machines, he has never seen that happen."

"Jesus. Did he fix it?"

"No," Lisa replied. "They of course had to order a new one. He wanted to come back next Monday to fix it but I asked if he could do it any sooner. I knew we had that counseling appointment and told him that I had Fridays off too. So he is going to be able to come this Friday. This whole week without a washing machine though, what a pain. I'm glad it's still under warranty though."

Calvin took a deep breath. Since she had mentioned the counseling, he thought that now was as good a time as any to bring up that he really did not intend on going after all.

Do not fall from grace, he chanted to himself.

"Lisa, I can't go to that. It wouldn't be right."

"OH MY God!" she exclaimed, "Are you seriously flip flopping on that again!? After 12 years together you can't give me an hour with a counselor!? You know that there is really no hope of fixing this without some outside help don't you?"

He took another deep, slow breath and said what's been on his mind for quite some time now.

"I don't see this marriage working out. The first thing a counselor is going to ask us is if we both want to be there and work toward fixing the marriage. I can't honestly answer yes to that question."

Her response came furious and fast.

"So let me ask you the question since you appear to be too much of a pussy to say it. Do you want a divorce?" she asked.

The word 'divorce' rang throughout his head. The stigma associated with it produced images he didn't want to deal with. But, the word was his reality. While he in no way thought he'd have this conversation today, especially on the phone under a downtown overpass next to a fast-food joint, he answered her.

"Yes," he said, "I want a divorce."

Lisa broke into hysterical sobs over the phone.

"You piece of shit! Really?! I can't believe you are willing to throw away so many years of our lives just like that! And for no real reason!" she screamed.

He cried now too.

"This is obviously not getting better Lisa, it's not fair to you to keep stringing you along like this. I think it's just time we end it," he said quietly.

"How could you do this to me? I absolutely hate you for doing this to me!"

With tears steaming down his face, he wanted to try and salvage something from her. He was afraid he'd never see his kids again. What if she left, and just disappeared for good?

"I want us to be able to be amicable, even to be friends. I still love you Lisa, and I want a relationship with you. The kids mean the world to me, they are my everything, I can't lose them."

"Oh, but you just don't want to be married to me anymore. But you still want to be my friend!? No. No way, Calvin. I'll never want to even see you again! How could you even have the balls to say that you still love me? Whatever. You have no idea how much you've hurt me."

She paused, then said, "Maybe you will end up with the kids full time... would you want that? Maybe I just can't be here anymore."

Is this what he really wanted? It was too late to back down now. He told himself he needed to stay strong, that he needed to keep his backbone.

"I trust you enough Lisa, that you wouldn't do that to our kids. You love them too much. I'm truly sorry for doing this to you. Truly, I am."

"Goodbye Calvin," she said, and hung up her phone. He laid his head back on the headrest and closed his eyes.

"It's done," he said to himself, proud for sticking to what he wanted and not backing down this time.

"I did it," he said aloud, with a hint of a smile forming under his tear-stained cheeks.

He was composed enough to get through the rest of the afternoon at work, and headed home at promptly 4 o'clock. About two miles from home, he noticed an SUV that looked a lot like Lisa's Honda heading toward him. As it got closer, he noticed it was her behind the wheel. They both pulled over, and rolled down their windows to talk.

"I'm taking Sterling to the ER," she said, "He still hasn't kept anything down all day. It's been too long, I need to take care of my son."

"I'll come," he said and pulled a U-turn and followed Lisa to the ER.

Sterling was brought back right away and set up in a room with an IV. The nurse said the doctor would be in shortly, and left the four of them alone. Lisa and Calvin sat on opposite sides of the hospital bed, both looking down at their little boy. Hannah sat on Calvin's lap.

"You still sure you want to do this?" said Lisa, who looked like she'd been crying since their conversation.

"This isn't the time to talk about it," he said, "But I'm sure. For now, let's get our little boy healthy."

"You know he's picking up on all this, right? This is why he's sick. The stress is physically making him ill," said Lisa.

"I guess the sooner we get this over with the sooner he can start to recover."

Chapter 24
The Pull of Comfort
Saturday, February 25, 2006

The rest of the workweek was awkward, to say the least. Calvin and Lisa both seemed to go through the motions of existing day-to-day, knowing their marriage was over but not sure how to take the next steps. Calvin argued that he should live there until they could work out the details of the divorce. Lisa disagreed, but neither made the move to make it official. They continued sleeping in the same bed, though without emotion or even conversation. Eventually Lisa brought up the counseling appointment on Monday. They hadn't talked much during the week about their explosive divorce conversation last Monday. The issue with Sterling's sickness and the emergency room visit had pushed that under the rug.

"Calvin, remember that I scheduled that counseling appointment on Monday... Why don't we just give it a chance and see what the counselor has to say? I want to make sure that when our children get older and ask me about our divorce, I can look them in the eye and tell them exactly why our marriage fell apart. What I don't want to say is, 'Your dad gave up and decided that he didn't want to be married anymore.' I want to tell them that I worked like hell, we went to counseling, and that we did all that we could to stay married but that in the end we decided to part ways. Right now I couldn't say that. And without meaning to be negative, there would be quite the negative picture of their father found in that truth."

Calvin had already checked out of the marriage. Going to counseling would only offer a Lisa a false hope, which he didn't want to give her.

"Lisa, I can't do counseling, and that has nothing to do with the kids. If I had my way I'd take them full time. I love them more than anything and they'll always feel that. This is about us... you deserve the chance to find your true love. You're such a loving mom and a wonderful person, you're just not MY person."

She went berserk.

"You said you'd try!" she said furiously.

Her eyes harbored an anger he'd never seen in her. "And why the hell won't you!?"

"I feel like the only reason for going to counseling would be to help you understand my position, not to save our marriage. I can't go with that intent, it's not fair to you."

Sobbing now, yet completely enraged, she pounded on his chest with her fists, saying between sobs, "I hate you! I hate you for doing this to us! How could you do this to me? You're ruining our life!"

"I've done this for too long," she growled, "I'm done! I'm finished being dragged along by you and being treated like shit by you. I'm done with you!"

With that, Lisa stormed into their walk-in closet and grabbed handfuls of Calvin's clothes off the racks, still on their hangers and threw them down into a pile on the bedroom floor.

When the closet was empty, Lisa moved to his dresser drawers and dumped the contents into a handful of garbage sacks she had grabbed from the kitchen. It didn't take even ten minutes before she had all of his clothes in piles and sacks. One more glance around assured Lisa that she had everything. She grabbed the piles and started dragging them across the house and to the waiting Audi in the garage. She popped the trunk and shoved his belongings inside, cracking some plastic hangers with the force of her rage as she went. Lisa was indeed on a rampage, marching in and out of the garage.

...

Calvin stood silent watch. It was finally happening. He was emotionless until he caught sight of Sterling standing and watching from a distance. The child had woken up from his nap and stood silently in the doorway to his bedroom. He watched his mother ferociously drag things down the hall and into the garage without any thought to how the children might react to her rage.
Calvin saw the sad look on his face, but could also see that he was trying to be brave. Smart beyond his four years, Sterling beyond a doubt knew that his daddy was moving out, without anyone even telling him so. "Sterling honey, come here," Calvin said, motioning him over with his arm.
Sterling approached the living room, and Calvin kneeled down to his level and looked him in the eyes.

"Honey, know I'll always love you okay? I'm not going to be living here anymore, but I'll still see you all the time."

Saying those words out loud broke his heart, and he wanted to cry harder than ever. But he knew he couldn't let his son see that kind of a breakdown. His hands were resting on his son's tiny shoulders as Sterling looked into his father's eyes.

In his strongest voice possible, which was still uncontrollably shaky, Calvin said, "Sterling, you'll always be my little boy, and I'll always love you, okay? Always, no matter what. You are my life, and I'm going to make sure we see each other all the time, okay? I love you big boy."

Calvin couldn't hold in his tears anymore, and brought his son in for a hug. He squeezed him as hard as he ever had, not wanting to let him go. He knew that once he did, he'd never hug him as a live-in daddy again.

He left Sterling in the living room, deciding that he had better go and hug his baby girl before it was time to go. Her sleeping face looked beautiful and peaceful against her bright pink pillowcase.

Her curls made a little halo around her head; his princess.

Calvin didn't know how to properly process what was happening; how he could not be with these children every day? But the winds were in motion and there was no stopping this cyclone now. He kissed his daughter, inhaled her soft baby scent and turned to leave her room.

With the car loaded, Lisa stood waiting in the living room by Sterling's side. Clearly furious, she huffed in quick breaths and couldn't control her crying. Calvin knew the time had come to go, and with one final squeeze, he said one last, 'I love you,' to Sterling and walked out into the garage.

Lisa followed him to the doorway of the laundry room. She had taken the garage door opener out of the car and the house and mailbox keys off his key ring. She reached out and handed him the car key, then turned to go back into the house. Turning abruptly back toward him again, she quickly moved down the two steps to the garage floor and over to him. He paused at the open door of his car.

She reached for his left hand, grabbed his wedding ring and pulled it off his finger. It came off surprisingly easy.

"If you don't want to be married anymore, you shouldn't be wearing it. It's a lie to have this ring on. We made a vow to each other. I meant that when I said it, obviously you didn't. You can't even give me one hour in counseling. Do you even have anything to say Calvin?"

He looked her in the eyes, and paused briefly.

"No."

He was absolutely speechless. It was almost like he was watching this happen to someone else. He felt like he was in a fog. He looked down at his bare ring finger and suddenly felt very sad.

"Very poetic for the best copywriter in town. Nice. You have no garage door opener, no mailbox key, no house key, and no Honda key. Know that you'll never step foot in this house again. This is no longer your home."

With that, she walked away and shut the door to the house. He heard the click of the deadbolt and stood alone in the garage. Slowly he sank into the supple driver's seat, started the car, and backed out of the garage for the last time.

The only place he thought to go, with all of his belongings, was back to his mom and dad's house. He didn't want to spend money on a hotel room, not when he and Lisa were going to be dividing finances and trying to figure out if she was going to keep the house or not.

He just wasn't ready to head to his parents' house and face them, so he drove toward his office where he knew he could reflect in silence. On the way he called Elizabeth to let her know what happened. They cried together on the phone, but reassured each other that through the pain, new paths would open.

"I think I'm in shock, Elizabeth," he said, "I can't believe it actually happened. Just three months ago I would have never guessed I'd be in this situation."

"It's amazing how quickly a life's path can be altered by the incredible complex simplicity of choice, isn't it? Just make sure this is your truth, Cal," Elizabeth said.

"It feels right," he replied, "I mean, it hurts, bad...and the thought of not living with my kids anymore... my God... it breaks my heart..."

He choked up and couldn't get any more words past the growing lump in his throat.

"You're going to keep being an incredible father to them Cal. Maybe even better than ever," Elizabeth said reassuringly.

"I know, you're right. Good Lord Elizabeth... I'm so glad we're going through this together."

He continued, "I just don't think I would have ever done it had I never met you. And Christ, this all happened within three months. That's still baffling to me. Three months and I am a completely different person. Wow."

He paused for a moment before continuing.

"Well, I guess I'm going back to Mom and Dad's basement again. Hey, maybe I'll see the lights again, the ones I saw when I was a kid down there..."

"Seriously Cal," Elizabeth replied, "I have a feeling you know them pretty well by now."

He chuckled at the realization that the lights all those years were Seneda, Seamus, Jade, maybe even Him and Her. It was comforting. And a little embarrassing that he hadn't made that simple connection earlier.

"Just know, Cal, that you and I can't start anything right away. If we're meant to be, we'll know when it's our time. I still have my marriage issues to work out. I do love you. And I'm here for you, always."

"I love you too... thank you."

The conversation with Elizabeth made him feel better. While at his office, he called his parents, getting their voicemail. He left a message, saying that Lisa had kicked him out and he'd be downstairs in their spare bedroom by morning.

He spent the next few hours alone in his office, crying. He didn't leave until nearly midnight, then drove to his new temporary home in the basement he knew so well.

Chapter 25
Fall From Grace
Sunday, February 26, 2006

Calvin woke feeling strong and ready to begin
putting together the pieces and beginning his new
life. The first thing he had to do was get out of his
parents' house and find an apartment. He'd never
lived on his own, and the thought of having an
apartment to himself was, admittedly, exciting.
Upstairs, his dad milled around the kitchen trying to
find mundane tasks to do, which he'd often do when
he was upset. It looked like he was trying to get some
sort of a breakfast cooked while reorganizing the
pots and pans drawer. Calvin turned the corner and
saw his dad, immediately recognizing the concerned
and stressed facial expression he wore.
"Hey Dad," he said quietly.
He looked at his son, his face transforming from
stressed to sorrowful. Calvin could see tears welling
in his dad's eyes.
"Good morning," he said, hugging him, "I didn't
think this would actually happen. If a divorce
happens, your mom and I will be here for you."
Mom entered the room as Dad finished, and began
to cry.
"Oh honey," she said, "I'm so sorry. What
happened?"

"I've just... well, I've been wondering if I made the right choice in getting married so young for years now. I've just kept it hidden and not talked about it. But, Mom, I've learned a lot about truth lately, and making sure I live life the way I want to live. I said some really hard things to Lisa. Really hard. And you know, I'm proud of myself. I never thought this would happen either. Not in a million years. But it did, and it feels right."

"Okay honey... it's just... the babies. What if Lisa takes them and we don't get to see them anymore?" Mom began crying again.

"I'll do whatever I have to, to make sure that doesn't happen. I'm sure Lisa loves the kids enough to keep the stability of their grandparents through all this. This isn't going to be easy, but it's right, okay Mom?" She nodded and hugged him.

"Thanks for letting me stay here," he said, "I promise I won't stay long. I'm going to shop for apartments today and even look into trading in my car. I'm gonna have to get rid of some payments and live pretty cheaply."

With that, he excused himself and left the house to go find a new home.

Being a Sunday, the offices at any apartment building he was interested in were closed. He did manage to get a hold of a woman on the phone, who said she wasn't able to show him any units until the middle of the week.

Something he didn't expect happened when he told that lady that he was in the middle of a divorce. The word echoed in his head, as images of his wife and their life together passed through his mind.

For the first time since he was kicked out of the house, he felt like he may have made a horrendous mistake. But was it too late? Or was this just a moment of weakness he needed to will himself through?

Chapter 26
The Last Gift
Monday, February 27, 2006

Calvin woke Monday morning feeling better than on Sunday, though the reality of waking alone in his parents' basement was another brutal slap in the face. He hurriedly dressed and left, anxious for the distractions of work.

He should have known what awaited him there. Or rather, whom. Just as he sat down and prepared to open his email, he caught the familiar glimmer from the corner of his eye.

"A moment?" he heard Him say.

"For you, of course," Calvin said, "I should have known I'd be hearing from you today. I could use it. I just keep thinking to myself, like you said before... do not fall from grace."

"And what do you think of that?" He said.

"I think it tells me I'm headed in the right direction, and I must stay the course. Stay true to myself. And that it will be very difficult, considering you even had a difficult time."

"But for different reasons," He said, "And why would it be that my time as a man would make me any different in strength than you?"

Calvin paused, taking this to mean that even as a man, he wasn't any more superior to any other human. He was just that... a human.

"I only know a little bit about your struggles, though I know mine and that's all that matters right now."

"Good," He said, "Say the words. Fall from grace."

"Fall from grace."

"What is grace to you?" He asked.

Calvin felt like this may be a test, to see what he'd learned. He strained his mind, trying to keep his thinking clear and simple.

"Grace is just honesty," he finally said, "And truth to myself and those I love."

"I am listening to you as you find your path. I am with you. Keep sorting," He said, reassuringly.

And then it hit him.

"Truth to myself."

Not to Elizabeth, not to Seamus, not even to Them.

He wondered how he'd let things get this far with Lisa, yet he knew the answer was because he thought that's what they all wanted to happen. Maybe he'd been trying to make THEM happy. But what about him? What about what Calvin wanted?

"What if I'm supposed to stay with Lisa for now," he urgently said, finally speaking aloud, "Could this all have been a test to see if I would leave? That by caving to the pressure, to the temptation of something more, that I would fall from grace?"

"Continue," He responded, "What is your reasoning for that being your grace?"

"My heart was content there. Being away from that comfort hurts. What if my grace is with her and with our amazing children there?"

"Why do you sum total your grace with three entities?" He said, "You are still falling into the trap. Not giving full light and love to each entity with good grace. In a willing manner. Yes, grace is truth. What it is not is the muddled definition of honoring and favoring. The dictionary might tell you it means to give beauty and elegance or charm to something. However, society's view of grace is misconstrued by their concept of life and living. Think about that statement."

Calvin nodded as he tried to follow the eloquent path of words laid before him.

He continued, "To stay in good graces to most means to eat crow and appear to be happy. To be cordial and appear to be the best you can. If you break it down, and take beauty, elegance, and charm individually, that definition is correct...but only with the proper sight. Beauty... what brings beauty?"

Calvin realized that was now a question to him.

"What brings beauty..." he repeated, stumped by the seemingly simple question. "Truth, I suppose. Light. And confidence."

"Absolutely," He said, "Less you forget love. Love is beauty. You know your kids are wonderful. Yet if you don't have absolute love for them you demean and negate to see their beauty. But if there is not truth IN their love, then there is no truth indeed."

"So that is why to others, my kids are just 'wonderful kids.' To me we see absolute love. As all parents do."

"Yes," He said.

"So now let's take elegance," He continued, "What is elegance? To them and to you."

"What is elegance," he repeated again, as he thought about it. "Elegance is typified in beauty. It's high-class. It's a certain pride. And again, it's confidence."
"And to them? Meaning society in general?" He asked.
"To them," he said, "Elegance is sometimes lavished in extravagance. A synonym for money, even."
"Very good. And lastly charm..." He said, not even needing to pose this one as a question.
Calvin answered quickly this time. "Charm is also truth. If there is truth in a person, and there is confidence in how he or she speaks, there is charm. But to them... to society, charm too often is falsity. It is lies. To 'turn on the charm.' There's either charm or there isn't."
"So what does it mean to fall from grace?" He asked.
Calvin knew the answer immediately, and now it seemed so simple.
"Falling from grace means to fall into society's view of grace, and not be true to what I know. To live for others' happiness. To act in a way that others expect, or want, me to act."
"So the question remains," He said, "Do you strive for their grace or your own?
"My own," he said.
"Do my words, 'Don't fall from grace,' have more meaning now?" He asked.
"Of all the things you told me those are the words I am holding onto most. Yes, they hold more meaning now."
"Do they hold clear meaning now?" He asked.
"Yes."

"So why would we test you to see if you should stay with Lisa? And in this manner?" He asked, "Why wouldn't we just take her away from you?"

Calvin didn't respond.

"Isn't it the fear of losing something that makes us cling more than anything? I just tell you that there are consequences to falling from grace..."

Calvin nodded again.

"...And more so for not knowing what grace is," He said, "Simple words, simple principles. Go now... in love and peace."

The roller coaster in Calvin's head hit its apex. He fluctuated from being confident that he wanted back with Lisa to believing the easier solution would be going through with the divorce. The conversation with Him was reassuring, in that he fully realized that whatever choice he made, the choice was his alone. No pressure. No wrong choice. As long as it was the choice that he really wanted.

These thoughts made getting through another workday difficult. There were times he just had to laugh to himself, wondering what his employees and co-workers would think if they knew he'd been talking to 'God' all this time while locked in his office. Talk about a one-way ticket to the looney bin. It sure made the drama of ad agency life seem trivial though. He was actually amazed he ever devoted the majority of his time and energy to it. If he ever got his wife back, or ended up with a new one someday, he vowed right there to make sure his priorities were in the right place.

With his mind halfway in his work and halfway on his grace, an e-mail appeared in his inbox. The sender field was blank, but the subject line is what caught his attention. It wasn't just a period this time. It had a title:

Subject: Last Gift

He hurriedly opened the email, and read it straight through.

"Because this well may be my last gift to you, I shall make it worthy. This knowledge I impart to you with love and with honor.
Upon my fall from grace, or in Her eyes my near fall from grace, I lost my honor and my purpose. For true love I lost my physical body and thusly an heir was to be made to carry out the evolution and teachings of existence, truth and love. This heir was an incredibly special being. Worthy of glory, worthy of his fame, worthy of declaring that he truly lived, that he truly loved.
Worthy until the day he fell from grace.
As we know heirs are created with consorts in hand. The balance is made and, with trust by their Creator they are meant to walk hand-in-hand into existence teaching and spreading the knowledge of truth and love. They are designed to touch hearts and to start epidemics of positive evolution. They are prepared before existence for extraordinary acts and rightful places of greatness in the seats of enlightenment. You will know an heir by their hearts, their words, their actions, and their eyes. You will know an heir by the feeling you get looking into a reflection of truth and of pure love.

My first heir was named Jesus Christ. Many stories have been told, many a lore written, and many a war have been fought in his name. Souls have followed him near and far to hear his teachings and to feel his love. Myriads of beings can attest to his healing powers and purity of love. What most don't have the privy of knowing is how truly human Christ became.

Through his life he struggled with his gifts, with his position in life. To know at such a young age what destiny awaits can be most trying. He was as dedicated as I've ever seen. His will and intent unmatched and his heart as pure as the white sands he walked upon. Day and night my heir toiled to become a better being, minute-by-minute yearning to teach more, to touch more lives. All the while my heir felt the ache inside. He searched far and wide on his travels for what would fill this emptiness. For a long while he thought it was that he wasn't seeking truth enough. For an even longer while, he thought perhaps his will just wasn't potent enough. Then one day a being walked into his life and changed him forever.

To most, she was a common street rat and whore. Though most looked down upon her for her social status, there was not one alive who could honestly admit to hating her. In fact all who took the chance of knowing her loved her instantly. The warmth that seeped from her eyes and the energy that filled every heart standing next to her was breathtaking. At first glance she wasn't a striking beauty. Her status was only due to skewed eyes of the blurry-eyed society. Upon deeper inspection one would be quite taken with her. Her delicate features, her pristine skin; She was the quintessence of what it was to be a woman. She was the epitome of femininity. It took one glance for Christ to lose his breath and for the ages of aching in him to be filled.

The first test my consort and I put before them was to see if the connection designed before them was strong enough. We tested Christ's will against society's intent. I'm sure you know of the infamous task of which we speak.

"Let he who hath no sin cast the first stone."

She was about to be stoned to death for being a prostitute. Christ, seeing this and feeling the love in his heart, and the need to teach of truth and love said to the masses...

"Let he who hath no sin cast the first stone."

This floored the blood hungry crowd. They were compelled to stop and think of his words. To absorb the fact that, though in their eyes this girl was a social pariah and a testament to all that is negative and dirty, they themselves were no better. Their will and intent was not what it should be and thusly they had no right to harm her in any way. They also had to stand before a man whose will and intent was flawless. Being that he was the only one who had the right to cast the stone yet chose not to resonated within them for ages and forever changed them.

Life carried on and they walked hand in hand, heart to heart. They were the closest two spirits have ever been. Their minds, souls, and bodies synchronized to perfection. They were happiness. They were love. They... were.

The downside of their story is the fact that she had to be kept in the shadows. I say "had to" loosely because it, like all things, was a choice. Christ by this time had status. He had followers, friends, and family who looked up to him. He had an image to uphold and opinions to not falter. He had minds and beliefs to not disappoint. Slowly but surely Christ began to lose sight of what was truly important. He began to cling to the comfort that his followers brought. The adoration and respect they bestowed. Though she was his equal and his consort, Christ couldn't get past the fear of the opinions of those closest to him. He let his false pride and his self-induced concept of grace distort his true intent. He began to lose sight of himself and his right to happiness, his destiny for truth. He began to live for others and for their truth. He became a martyr.

Sadly, in his last days Christ battled. Forty days and forty nights walking through the desert. Lonely, starving, and aching for the comforts and the nostalgia of his supporters. He battled temptation daily at the hands of Samael and his minions. Until finally Christ could no longer take the pressure of being an heir. He could no longer see clearly will and intent. He had no concept of true love. All he could think of was making others happy. What he didn't know was that he was truly about to sacrifice himself like a lamb. And for what? That is a question I still ask myself daily.

Christ was crucified. He thought he gave himself in full to those he loved, and those to come for ages.

Truthfully, he died in vain thinking that he had found his grace by giving it up for the sake of others' happiness.

What he neglected to see was that he was just falling from grace. Had he lasted longer, had he kept clear vision and clear intent, pure will, he would have done much greater things. Instead chaos, hatred, and war ensued for years afterwards. His truth, his life, was muddied through words of fear. And the light upon his consort and her equally amazing story was lost.

So then what after Christ you ask?

Another heir was born. Many ages later. To this day he faces the same battles, the same trials, and the same heart aches. Will he falter? That is to be seen. No matter which path he chooses he must know that he is loved. He must know that he is supported. He must know his consort lives parallel, for now unseen. And he must know, it is his right to go whichever way he must.

Christ, upon his death, uttered a quote that has filled the ears of many. They are words that to this day strike pain and pity in his followers. They are words today that I will explain, in truth and not the way the "holy text" would have you see.

Christ's life was blessed in more ways than one. He was gifted with the ability to hear truth, to hear my words. However, when Christ was to the point of his final trials I had no choice but to sit back silently. I had to let his own will and intent be formed. I had to let him make his choices without pressure. He had become so comfortable in hearing truth from the source that he stopped seeking truth. He stopped working for the right to exist in the manner he did. I was left with no alternative but to sit back and watch him in the shadows while he struggled through his time. As much as it pained me to see him hurt and cry, as difficult as it was to let him make wrong choice after wrong choice, I did what true love and knowledge required. I let him exist. I let him experience. In trust and unconditional love, I let him make the ultimate choice to walk the path he did. And the day he shouted with tears in his eyes,
"My God why hast thou forsaken me?"
I cried.
The consequence of choice is existence.
So as we approach the day that most call "Ash Wednesday," the start of lent, the memory of Christ's battle, I say that I will watch you my heir. For forty days and forty nights in silence, with love, and with trust.
With true love unconditionally
I AM

Chapter 27
Reflection
Monday, February 27, 2006

"My God..." Calvin uttered aloud in a drawn out whisper.

He stared into his screen blankly before reading the message over and over. The enormity of it was completely overwhelming. Tears flooded his eyes as he read it for the fourth time, his hand clasped over his mouth. His heart pounded. This message... he was alternating his thinking between what it meant to him as an individual and at the same time knew it could literally change the way Christianity is perceived throughout the world. But how could he possibly even begin to spread this message? Would anyone even believe him?

He thought about the previous three months, and knew it was all a path leading to this moment; to learning this extraordinary piece of information. Everything up to this point was a series of choices to see if he could even get here, or if he'd choose to ignore it all. And now, he was about to face 40 days of no contact and no advice, in a time when he thought he'd need it most.

But, he thought, that was exactly the point. It was time he thought for himself. As He said, even Christ struggled with "too much truth from the source."

Now that he had been stripped to the very core of who he was, he had a chance to rebuild, with truth and grace. And he had 40 days to figure out where his true desires lay, and to live up to the truths he'd created over the last few months. He was almost feeling like he had it easy, having Samael out of the way. After all, Christ had to deal with him AND being alone in the harsh and desolate desert. Of course, now he had the decision of whether or not to go through with a divorce. He might have preferred the desert.

Would it just be easier to begin rebuilding his marriage? But if he did...who was this consort if it wasn't Elizabeth? When would they meet?

Calvin's thoughts didn't deviate from the Last Gift for the rest of the day.

Jesus Christ fell from grace...

He repeated it to himself over and over... it all made so much sense, but at the same time was contrary to everything he'd ever heard. It just made Christ so... human. No doubt he was a great man in life, but even he couldn't live his truth. In essence, he chose to die for others instead of living for himself... a harsh reminder of the decision Calvin faced today. That, according to the conversation with Him earlier that day, was the exact definition of falling from grace.

And now it's my turn...

He couldn't keep his thoughts going in one direction for more than a few seconds at a time. He struggled with being called the next heir of Him, and being compared with, or at least treated as an equal, to Christ himself.

If people thought he was arrogant before, what would they think if they heard him say that?

The power of His words continued to echo in his mind...

"... This knowledge I impart to you with love and with honor."

"...My first heir was named Jesus Christ. Many stories have been told, many a lore written, and many a war have been fought in his name."

"...he let his false pride and his self induced concept of grace distort his true intent. He began to lose sight of himself and his right to happiness, his destiny for truth. He began to live for others and for their truth. He became a martyr."

"...Christ could no longer take the pressure of being an heir. He could no longer see clearly will and intent. He had no concept of true love."

"No concept of true love," he repeated, "Do I? Would staying with Lisa be what would make other people happy, or make me happy?"

"...he died in vain thinking that he had found his grace by giving it up for the sake of others' happiness. What he neglected to see was that he truly was only falling from grace. Had he lasted longer, had he kept clear vision and clear intent, pure will, he would have done much greater things. Instead chaos, hatred and war ensued for years afterwards."

"My God," Calvin said aloud, "The things he could have done had he lasted longer... instead of wars **fought** in his name, maybe Earth would have seen unconditional peace **accepted** in his name."

Still, the power of this incredible message floored him.

"...he was truly about to sacrifice himself like a lamb. And for what? That is a question I still ask myself daily."

Calvin knew that publicly saying Christ was sacrificed like a lamb, and for nothing, would essentially get him crucified in the eyes of modern society. But it was truth. And what made it even more incredible was that the words were coming directly from the God they worshipped.

"...So then what after Christ you ask? Another heir was born. Many ages later. To this day he faces the same battles, the same trials and the same heart aches. Will he falter? That is to be seen."

Incredible. 'Another heir was born...' could that really be him? And how could he possibly manage to spread light where even Christ failed?"

"...Christ upon his death uttered a quote that has filled the ears of many. They are words that to this day strike pain and pity in his followers. They are words today that I will explain, in truth and not the way the "holy text" would have you see."

Calvin was absolutely delighted that He put 'holy text' in quotes. It was proof to him that even God himself doesn't believe the Bible is the literal truth.

"...As much as it pained me to see him hurt and cry, as difficult as it was to let him make wrong choice after wrong choice, I did what true love and knowledge required. I let him exist. I let him experience. In trust and unconditional love, I let him make the ultimate choice to walk the path he did. And the day he shouted with tears in his eyes; 'My God why hast thou forsaken me?' I cried."

Calvin realized THAT'S where the problem with religion stemmed. God doesn't direct our lives, he simply observes, and hopes we make the right choices. His gift to all humans is simply the gift of being alive, and having the ability to make those choices. Even if, as in Christ's life, those choices are wrong.

"...I will watch you my heir. For forty days and forty nights in silence, with love, and with trust."

"I can do this," he thought, "I just need to find my balance, find my truth, and live them."

His words took Calvin all the way through the workday and into the evening in his basement room, his mind still spinning but now exhausted. He couldn't help but wonder if the Last Gift would actually be the last time he heard from Him. If he fell from grace, it probably would be.

He switched on the television to try and pull his mind from the Last Gift and quickly fell asleep.

Chapter 28
Heirs
Tuesday, February 28, 2006

Calvin stumbled through his day at work, his mind nowhere near the world of advertising. His thoughts were still clouded by the enormity of His words, the confusion about trying to get his family back, and the new thought of knowing he had to pretty much sever ties with Elizabeth. If she wasn't his consort, who was?

It didn't matter.

He couldn't let that influence his decision. Part of him wondered if he should go back to Lisa and his kids to bide time until he met the woman who was meant for him... If it wasn't too late.

Calvin didn't hear from Lisa, but did receive an email from Elizabeth, asking to see him later.

"What the hell," he said aloud, "I've got nothing else to do."

They met for dinner at a Chinese restaurant directly after work. His mind hadn't cleared all day, and Elizabeth could tell.

"You okay, Cal?" she asked.

"I don't know," he answered softly, "I'm struggling honestly. Bad. I feel like I've hit the bottom. Like I've completely crumbled. Like I don't know who I am anymore. I feel like I've lost everything I've ever known..."

His voice trailed off.

"Yeah. It's definitely time to start rebuilding," she said, "You have crumbled. You've been through a lot; you've been given the kind of knowledge that could overwhelm any human. But you were chosen for a reason. Because you are strong, and you can handle it. You'll rebuild, and be a more beautiful, and influential, human than ever. No matter how hard it is right now."

He nodded, knowing he needed to hear her encouragement tonight. She was always able to make him feel better.

"Let's go get some drinks," he said after he paid the waitress.

Surely some alcohol would help make him feel better.

They went to the familiar surroundings of The Rail, and sat at their upstairs table. He ordered his usual Jack and Coke. As he was sipping on his second drink, Elizabeth put her hand on his shoulder.

"Cal, you've hardly said a word since we've been here," she said, "You're not yourself tonight."

She paused as her eyes welled with tears.

"And I think I know why. You've made your decision, haven't you? You need to let me go. It's okay."

Elizabeth paused, then continued, "I've been meaning to tell you... Jack and I talked and we're going to give things another try."

Calvin's heart sunk at the reality of not being able to pursue a relationship with Elizabeth, even though he knew now she wasn't the one for him. That didn't change the fact that he loved her though.

"This is so hard," Elizabeth said through tears, "But I know that's the way it has to be."

"But what about... us? Our connection?"

"We've made our choices Calvin. We did what we had to do. You don't need me. And that's what all this is about anyway, right? Figuring out what you really want and need in life? I know our connection wasn't meant as true love, it had a different purpose, but I do hope you find love one day..."

"I'll miss you terribly," she continued as she began to cry, "But I'll survive."

"You know, if we do this right, we could stay in each other's lives," Calvin said.

"And watch you, always wondering what it could've been like?" asked Elizabeth.

Calvin knew that Elizabeth was right.

Their story together had ended.

"But even so," she continued, "You will do great things Calvin Janek. You ARE great things. Love your grace. Embrace it. Teach, love, and touch..."

Her last words were said in a fading voice, and he knew what was coming.

"Git..." said Seamus through Elizabeth, in his familiar Irish accent.

"Wow," he said, surprised to hear from his old friend Seamus, "It's been quite a while..."

"Aye, now ye know who I've been competin' with for time with ye," said Seamus, which made him smile. He continued, "And I've been watchin' ye. And I know ye be needin' a brother right now. By the way, did ye like my handy work?"

"Handy work? What do you mean?"

"With yer washin' machine. I figured ye could use a little time to yerself," he said.

"That was you!? The repair guy said he'd never seen that before. That was a big mess. Don't do that anymore."

"Okay, okay. So this is not a fun time. Not an easy time. It's hard to be faced with choices," Seamus said. "What ye do... is decide first what ye want," said Seamus.

"Which I've done," Calvin said, "At least, that's what I'm trying to do."

"Are ye trying, or are ye given in?" said Seamus, "Okay git, I'll level with ye. They will tell ye this and they will tell ye that. But what ye need to do is stay strong. Aye, They could give ye a map and a set destination, and that would be easy. But who said bein' an heir was easy?"

"Well, I've had a couple months to realize that sure as hell is not the case," Calvin replied.

"You've had lifetimes to realize," Seamus said.

"Okay, then I've known consciously for a few months. I've had to go through the denial, the acceptance, and the action of it. All within a few months?"

"Yes," said Seamus.

"Why?"

"Ye either accept it or ye don't," he replied, "Will it be easier in 10 years to grasp?"

"What do I even say to Lisa? I'll come back and tell her, 'Oh, by the way, apparently I'm the heir of God."

"Be careful talkin' about bein' the heir, because that cannot be fully understood by anyone who isn't. And maybe it can't even be understood by those who are."

"What do I even do being an heir? It's not like I'm the second coming of Jesus and will bring world peace and stop wars and save the world."

"Bein' an heir means that you are given such great prospects, git," said Seamus, "Things will open to ye like none other. And... given strong enough will and intent, you COULD have the power to stop wars." Seamus paused before finishing his thought.

"And Jesus isn't comin' back, git. Ye were sent instead."

The words made Calvin slow down and think but also wreaked havoc inside his head.

"Well what am I supposed to do with that!? I want to live up to this so badly. I just feel at times like I'm left holding this gift... but it's broken."

"Aye, I know it's hard git. And I'm sorry for the burden of yer existence," said Seamus.

He continued, "But ye must understand... Five thousand years of waiting and hopin' fer this one lifetime of maybes. Git, no one blames ye. And no one has ill will toward ye. Ye are a good spirit and ye are love. Remember, ye bound Samael, ye git. Now maybe yer kids need their father and someday, if ye make yerself open to it, you'll meet yer true love and be the greatest duo since that fookin Jew and his girl."

That made Calvin laugh. That's the kind of comment that made him like Seamus so much.

"Maybe the next heir should be more prepared," Calvin said, "I just do NOT want to mess this up. This is important to me."

"To prepare an heir is to rob them of their will and intent," replied Seamus.

"Look," he continued, "Ye know that yer truth is what ye make it...yer whole truth or the truth ye choose to live. Choice is a fookin pain in the neck."

"And with that," he continued, "I'll be able to rest. I see ye have made yer choice, at least for now. And no one holds a grudge or ill feeling for ye. True love is unconditional, and it's what we have for ye."

"I will go to rest eternally," he continued.

With that comment, he knew deep down that Seamus' path had been completed. His purpose was to guide Calvin to this point in life, and Seamus was no longer needed as a guide.

Calvin felt an incredible sadness and guilt well inside of him. Seamus had been a good friend, a funny friend, and a caring brother.

"Do not feel the pull of guilt, git," he said, "And mourn not for yer choices. It's been a great journey, none of us regret anythin'."

"But I don't want this to end, Seamus. I just don't know where to go from here."

"Then ye have shit in both hands git. Which shit can ye live with fer the rest of yer life?" asked Seamus.

"You'll continue to grow, to rebuild, to experience, and to love. Right now yer kids need the best guide they have... you, ye git. Love them like we love ye. Thanks fer the love, git, and fer the laughs," said Seamus.

All Calvin could manage to say through his tears was, "What a journey."

He tipped back his Jack and Coke in honor of his old friend.

"Know this," Seamus continued, "Though this journey ends, ye are still an amazin' human. Ye are the true heir. Ye will touch people by just bein' you. Know that ye have meant the world to me, and I don't regret one moment of it. I can rest sayin' that I have had meaning. My experience has been a full and valid one. And I can say I gave my all to love and knowledge."

"I love you, brother," Calvin said, knowing Seamus was about to leave, forever.

"Aye, love is all I have... and you soak me in it," he said.

Calvin could hardly see through the tears in his eyes. He knew this was the right thing to do, but cutting contact with Elizabeth, and the spirits who came through her, was heart wrenching. All he could do was hug her, hoping to hold on to it all for each remaining second.

"Thanks for everything you've done for me," he managed to say, "I'll never forget you."

"You might, you might not," Elizabeth said in a shaky voice, "Now, you need to go."

He didn't know if Seamus heard his last words, and that broke Calvin's heart. With Elizabeth back, he gave her one final squeeze, knowing this was it. As hard as this was, he knew for certain it had to be this way if he had any chance of rebuilding a life and eventually finding his true consort and his true love. Calvin let go of Elizabeth and, remembering the night she caught his eye for the first time, looked into hers for the last.

"I'll always love you," he said as he stood, turned from her, and walked into the light of his new world, confident that in 39 days he'd emerge as a worthy heir.

Made in the USA
Las Vegas, NV
12 February 2022

43828865R00166